HEAD
TO HEAD

Jennifer Manuel

James Lorimer & Company Ltd., Publishers
Toronto

For my friend Julie, whose strength and support and loyalty both
on and off the field showed me what it means to belong.
You are a true leader of the pack.

James Lorimer & Company Ltd., Publishers acknowledges funding support from
the Ontario Arts Council (OAC), an agency of the Government of Ontario. We
acknowledge the support of the Canada Council for the Arts, which last year
invested $153 million to bring the arts to Canadians throughout the country. This
project has been made possible in part by the Government of Canada and with the
support of Ontario Creates.

Cover design: Gwen North
Cover image: Shutterstock

9781459415409
eBook also available 9781459414297
Cataloguing data for the hardcover edition is available from Library and Archives Canada.

Library and Archives Canada Cataloguing in Publication (Paperback)

Title: Head to head / Jennifer Manuel.
Names: Manuel, Jennifer, author.
Series: Sports stories.
Description: Series statement: Sports stories
Identifiers: Canadiana (print) 20200203517 | Canadiana (ebook) 20200203630 |
ISBN 9781459414280 (softcover) | ISBN 9781459414297 (EPUB)
Classification: LCC PS8625.A69 H43 2020 | DDC jC813/.6—dc23

Published by:
James Lorimer &
Company Ltd., Publishers
117 Peter Street, Suite 304
Toronto, ON, Canada
M5V 0M3
www.lorimer.ca

Distributed in Canada by:
Formac Lorimer Books
5502 Atlantic Street
Halifax, NS, Canada
B3H 1G4

Distributed in the US by:
Lerner Publisher Services
1251 Washington Ave. N.
Minneapolis, MN, USA
55401
www.lernerbooks.com

Printed and bound in Canada.
Manufactured by Marquis in Toronto, Ontario in August 2020.
Job #355136

Contents

1 Leader of THE PACK

Emika Tanaka received a pass from forward Rosa Cruz and turned up the left wing. Emika sprinted, pushing the soccer ball ahead with her cleats. Wetness from the cold grass soaked her ankles. Out of the corner of her eye she could see a defender racing to cut her off.

"We're with you, Emika!" Rosa shouted. She and the other Victoria Wolves forwards streaked up the field.

The Oak Bay Lions defender closed the gap on Emika. Slowing down, Emika searched for someone open. All her midfielders were covered by Lions players. All her forwards, too. Even Rosa, although she was working hard to lose her check. Everyone was covered except Maram Kassab, but she was far away on the opposite wing.

The Lions defender lunged at the ball to steal it. Emika tapped it ahead with the inside of her foot. Stepping her leg over the ball, Emika kicked it with the outside of her other foot. The scissor move fooled the defender into going in the wrong direction.

Emika burst down the wing once again.

"Drive to the net! Drive to the net!" Emika's best friend, Jabira Kassab, was cheering from the sidelines.

The defender chased after Emika. Glancing across the field, Emika spotted Maram again. This time Maram had cut across the field toward the goal. She was just ahead of Rosa, open at the top of the eighteen-yard box.

But if I don't make the pass perfect, Emika worried, *Maram will glare at me, like she always does.*

Then Emika remembered what Rosa had said to her at the start of the season: "You and Maram might think you hate each other. But our team is a wolf pack. We stick together."

With a sudden twist of her hips, Emika booted the ball as hard as she could. It arced high above the field, spinning toward the centre of the goal area.

Out of breath, Emika slowed to a jog.

"Keep pushing to the net, Emika!" Coach Bella Garcia yelled.

Emika picked up the pace as she watched Maram beat a defender and race toward the bouncing ball. The goalkeeper paused for a second, then tried to get to the ball before Maram. They almost crashed into each other.

Leaping into the air, Maram kicked the ball over the goalkeeper's shoulder. As the goalkeeper spun around, she lost her footing and slid to the ground. Maram sped past her and drilled the ball at the net.

The ball rebounded hard off the crossbar — straight to Rosa. Maram crouched low, ready to help Rosa or get the rebound if Rosa missed, too.

But there would be no rebound. Rosa trapped the ball with her thigh and shot it into the open net.

"Goal!" Jabira yelled.

It was 3–1 Wolves.

As Rosa jogged toward the centre line, she patted the Lions goalkeeper on the shoulder. "Great effort, keeper, great effort."

Just like Rosa to cheer on everyone, Emika chuckled to herself. *Even the other team.*

Then Rosa turned and pointed at Emika. "Super cross! Way to set up the play! You're so good at sensing everyone on the field!"

Emika grinned with pride. Then her smile faded as she remembered that this was Rosa's last game with the Victoria Wolves. Next week Rosa would be moving to Vancouver with her family. Not only would Emika miss Rosa, but she also expected the team's six-game winning streak to come to an end. Worse yet, how could Emika and Maram play together without Rosa to push them past their differences?

Rosa is the best captain ever, Emika thought. *No one could ever lead the wolf pack better than Rosa.*

Rosa pointed at Maram and said, "Great shot."

Maram frowned. "I missed."

Rosa shrugged. "Did you walk off the field because you missed?"

"Of course not," Maram said.

"Of course not," Rosa said as they took their positions at centre line. "Missing isn't the end of the game. You stuck with it, like you always do. You sure set a great example for the rest of us, Maram. Right, Emika?"

Emika clenched her jaw. The last thing she wanted to do was say something nice about Maram. Everyone knew that they had never gotten along since they started playing together two years ago. Still, Emika didn't want to let Rosa down. She nodded. "Yup."

Maram acted as if she didn't hear Emika. "Thanks, Rosa."

Emika rolled her eyes. *That Maram is as cold as the wet grass*, she thought.

After the game, Jabira waited on the sidelines with a bowl of orange slices for the team. Jabira was the biggest cheerleader for the Wolves, and Maram's sister. Although Jabira loved soccer, she found it too much to be on a team of her own, because of her cerebral palsy. It made it a challenge for her to run for long.

Often Emika and Jabira passed the ball around in the park. Emika adored Jabira. She wished Jabira's sister could be more like her.

"Three to one! The winning streak continues!" Jabira said to Emika.

"Not for long," Emika said. "Not once Rosa's gone."

"Rosa's great," Jabira said. "But she's just one player."

Emika sighed. "She's not just one player. She's our captain. She's the best captain ever. She's the leader of the pack. She brings the whole team together."

Rosa reached around Emika and took an orange slice from Jabira's bowl. "Don't worry, Emika. I have the perfect plan for replacing me. I already ran it past Coach Garcia."

Emika looked at Rosa with doubt in her eyes.

"Trust me." Rosa smiled.

"I do." Emika smiled back.

Rosa nudged Emika's shoulder playfully. "Just don't forget it."

"I won't," Emika said.

"Promise?"

Emika gave a nod. "Promise."

2 Rosa's CHOICE

The following Tuesday, the Wolves practised in the pouring rain.

Often Jabira joined the team for parts of the practice. Today she ran next to Emika during warm-up.

"Watch out!" Emika laughed as Jabira stumbled sideways into Emika's path.

"Sorry," said Jabira. "These legs don't always do what I ask."

The Wolves jogged from one sideline to the other. Rosa was also there for one last practice with her team before her family was to move that Friday. All the players went at the same easy pace to warm up their muscles.

"No one ahead, no one behind," Rosa reminded everyone. "We warm up as a team."

Coach Garcia called the team over to the centre where cones were placed in a giant figure eight. Rain dripped off the end of her nose. "Dribbling warm-up. Use the inside and outside of your feet."

Emika grabbed a soccer ball and stood in line.

Jabira went ahead of Emika. Although Jabira finished the drill slowly, she dribbled with the outside of her cleat around the tight curve of cones for the first time.

"Way to go, Jabira," Emika said. "Nice footwork."

Kelly Vanier and Jusdeep Patel clapped for Jabira as well. Maram didn't say a word to her sister. In fact, she wasn't even watching.

Can't she be a little nicer to Jabira? Emika wondered.

Next, the team practised corner kicks. It had always been Emika's job to take the corner kick. Nearly every time, she managed to give the Wolves a good chance to score.

"Your follow-through is perfect now," Rosa had told her the month before. "That's why the ball goes so far. Your leg extends nice and high."

As Emika placed the ball on the ground to take her first kick, she checked where all the forwards were positioned. Then she raised her arm to signal the kick.

Her cleat snagged the ground as she swung her leg. The ball went low and bounced behind the net before reaching any of the players.

"You got this, Emika," Kelly clapped as Emika prepared to try again.

Emika's second attempt wasn't any better. It rolled along the ground into the goal area where Nina Samuelson easily booted it away from the forwards.

"That's okay," Rosa called out. "Stick with it, Emika!"

Emika went back to the corner. This time she extended her leg high. The ball sailed over the goal and out of bounds. All the players watched it without moving.

Emika tried three more times. Not once did the ball make it to the goal area.

"Argh!" Emika complained to herself out loud. "I give up!"

"I'd like to try a couple," Maram told Coach Garcia. "I've been practising."

"Go for it," Coach Garcia nodded.

"But I —" Emika was surprised. No one else had ever wanted to take the corner kicks before. Why now all of a sudden? What was Maram up to? Why had she been practising corner kicks, when it was Emika's job?

"Stand by the goal post nearest," Maram told Emika as she set the ball in the corner.

Emika felt a wave of heat flush her face. Maram was always telling her teammates what to do. Which plays to make. Where to stand on the field. When to pass short or long. Emika bit her tongue and turned away before she said something awful.

"Be good for the team to have more than one player to take the corner kicks," Rosa said as Emika jogged into the goal area. Then Rosa pointed at the goal post and said, "You're still in the game. We need you right there."

Emika tried not to think about missing so many corner kicks in a row. Or that Maram seemed to be trying to take her place. She stood by the post and focused on getting ready to score.

The rain started to fall even harder. Maram raised her arm. Some of the players jostled against each other. Others cut and turned into different spots, trying to lose their checks.

Maram belted the ball with a *thwack!* It soared high, then curved sharply toward the goal.

Emika braced herself. The ball started to drop. Emika shuffled two quick steps to the right. She leaped off one leg and clenched her fists. As the wet ball hit her forehead, she jerked her neck just enough to direct it into the net.

"Beautiful header, Emika!" Kelly said.

"That's what I'm talking about!" Rosa pointed at Emika. "That's using failure as your fuel!"

Emika cringed at that word. *Failure.* But it was a beautiful goal!

Rosa called over to Maram. "You sure have been practising. What a corner! My dad calls that a banana kick. Curves in the air like a banana."

Coach Garcia looked at Maram, then at Emika. "You two work well together," she said. She flashed a strange smile at Rosa.

Emika groaned under her breath. She wished it had been anyone but Maram at the other end of the play.

And what was with Coach's smile at Rosa? Like they knew a secret. It was the same look Emika's parents had shared before her fourteenth birthday last year. But that secret was a good one — they had surprised her with a golden retriever puppy named Sinclair.

At the end of the practice, Coach Garcia gathered the team for a quick meeting. "As we all know, Wolves," Coach Garcia said, "we are losing our captain this week. Rosa, you have done a great job of leading this team. We'll miss you."

"Here's to Rosa!" Emika hollered.

The whole team joined Emika in applause.

"I can't wait to play you in the Vancouver tournament, Rosa," said Jusdeep.

The rest of the team chimed in, agreeing and excited about seeing Rosa again.

"The tournament is only a few weeks away," said Coach Garcia, "and we'll need to have our captain replaced by then."

"We could have another team vote," Kelly suggested.

At the beginning of the season, Coach Garcia had handed out tiny slips of paper. Everyone on the team had written the name of the person they most wanted as captain. Everyone had voted for Rosa.

Coach Garcia shook her head. "No vote. Not this time."

"Why not?" Maram asked. "We *should* vote."

Coach Garcia let out a small sigh. "It's not that I don't trust you girls to make a good decision. You picked Rosa, after all. And she has been one of the best captains I've ever seen."

"I'm with Maram," said Jusdeep, "I think a team should vote for the captain."

"Sometimes," agreed Coach Garcia. "But sometimes when a team votes, it becomes nothing more than a contest for who's most popular. Our new captain has to be more than just someone everyone likes."

Kelly asked, "If we're not voting, then who is picking the new captain?"

"Me," said Coach Garcia. "And Rosa. We've thought of the perfect solution."

Emika took a squirt of water. "So who's the new captain?"

"Not *captain*," replied Coach Garcia. "*Captains.* I'm appointing co-captains."

The team fell silent. They looked around at each other as if trying to guess who had been chosen. Then they looked back at Coach Garcia.

Coach Garcia motioned to Rosa. "I'll let you do the honours."

"Your new co-captains," Rosa announced, "are Emika Tanaka and Maram Kassab."

3 BENDABLE

"Rosa is the best," Emika said, "but she and Coach Garcia have made a big mistake."

Emika, Jabira and Kelly made their way toward the food court in the Bay Centre in downtown Victoria.

"Here I was worrying that we'd start to lose games without Rosa," Emika went on. "This is going to be worse than I imagined. It's a disaster. There's no way I can be a captain with Maram."

"Maybe it will work out fine," Kelly shrugged.

Emika gave Kelly a look. "Did you see how she jumped in to take over my corner kicks? I bet she'll try to take over being captain, too. That's what she always does. Remember when she spent all summer practising throw-ins so she could take those? Or when she practised being a goalkeeper in case she could play in net instead of Jusdeep? She'll try to do it all by herself."

"No one has to do anything by themselves," Jabira said.

"We have our wolf pack. That's what Rosa always says."

"Besides," Kelly offered, "it's not just anyone who picked you to be co-captains. It's Rosa. And if Rosa thinks you two will make good co-captains, maybe she's onto something."

Jabira looked sideways at Emika as she spoke to Kelly. "I'd feel really important if somebody like Rosa picked me to be a captain, wouldn't you?"

Emika tingled with pride. *It does feel pretty special that Rosa chose me*, she thought.

"It'd be a big honour, for sure." Kelly also looked at Emika out of the corner of her eye. "If it were me, I wouldn't want to let Rosa down."

Emika raised her hand. "Okay, okay, I get it. I'll give it a shot. For Rosa."

"And for the wolf pack," Jabira added.

"And for the wolf pack," Emika agreed. "Let's hope Maram thinks the same."

"Give her a chance," Jabira said. "I think my sister might surprise you."

Emika forced herself to smile. How could Jabira ever think anything hopeful about her sister? After all, Maram treated Jabira as if she wasn't even there.

The girls reached the escalator in the mall. Emika and Kelly held Jabira by the elbows as they always did on the escalator. Sometimes Jabira had to struggle to get her left leg onto the moving steps.

"Whatever happened between you and Maram, anyway?" Kelly asked Emika as they floated up to the second level.

Emika thought about it. What *had* happened between her and Maram? Many times she'd tried to remember. But she could never put her finger on it.

"I know Maram isn't the smiley type —" Kelly glanced at Jabira. "No offence."

Jabira waved her hand. "That's okay. Maram isn't exactly a big party, I get it."

"And she kind of sticks to herself a lot," Kelly continued. "It's not like she's good friends with anyone on the team, but she mostly gets along with everyone."

"I don't know how," Emika said. "All she does is boss everybody around."

Kelly crinkled her eyebrows. "She does?"

"All the time!" Emika said.

"Never really noticed," Kelly said. "All I know is that you two seem like you'd rather eat bugs than talk to each other."

In the food court, they each ordered bubble tea from Loyaltea. Getting bubble tea after their soccer practices had been their ritual since they had started playing for the Wolves. They sat at an empty table.

Jabira sighed. "They forgot my bendable straw." She went back to the counter and returned with a plastic straw.

"Plastic straws have been banned in Victoria, haven't they?" Kelly asked.

Jabira nodded as she slowly lowered her face to the bent straw and took a sip. "Mmm, lychee, the best! They passed the ban without asking people who have disabilities. They didn't realize that some of us need straws to be able to drink. But all food places are required to give me a bendable straw if I ask for one."

"Why does it have to be bendable?" Emika asked after taking a sip of her mango tea.

"Makes it easier for me to get my mouth to the straw." Jabira lifted her arms to show them the tremors in her fingers. "Would you trust these hands to not toss your bubble tea everywhere? I don't. So I learn to do things differently."

"Here's to bendable straws." Kelly raised her bubble tea and tapped the cup against Jabira's.

Emika's mind returned to practice. "Did you see everyone's face when Coach Garcia and Rosa made the announcement?"

"We all were surprised," Kelly said.

"Shocked, more like it," said Emika.

"Okay, shocked," agreed Kelly. "But only because it's not what anyone expected."

"No, it's more than that," said Emika. "They hate the idea of us being co-captains."

Jabira rolled her eyes. "Quit doubting yourself so much."

Emika ignored Jabira's comment. Then something occurred to Emika. "What if this is just a clever plan?" she asked.

Kelly crinkled her eyebrows. "Clever? How?"

"By making us co-captains," Emika explained, "Coach Garcia and Rosa think that we'll somehow become friends. You know, like in those cheesy movies?"

Jabira and Kelly both laughed at the idea and went back to drinking their tea.

Still, Emika wondered if it was true. If it was, Emika was right about one thing: Coach Garcia and Rosa had made a big mistake. Emika and Maram could never work together as co-captains. And they most certainly would never be friends.

★ ★ ★

After dinner, Emika headed downstairs to hang out with her older brother Kaito in his pottery studio. But as soon as she reached the basement, the doorbell rang. Sinclair barked at the sound. Emika rubbed behind the dog's ears before they both ran to the front door.

"Rosa!" Emika said when she opened the door. "Come in!"

"I can't stay," Rosa said.

Emika looked past Rosa to see Rosa's dad sitting in their car.

"I brought you a going-away present." Rosa handed Emika a small package wrapped in paper with little soccer balls all over it.

"Thank you, Rosa." Emika took the thin, rectangular gift. But you're the one going away. I should be giving you a gift."

"It's a special gift to help you with being captain," Rosa explained. "I just came from Maram's house. I gave one to her, too."

"Oh," Emika said. She tried to hide the disappointment in her voice. Somehow getting the same present as Maram made it feel less special.

Rosa got excited as she explained. "It's a book written by Abby Wambach. She was captain of the US women's soccer team. The book taught me to be a better captain." Rosa squinted an eye at Emika. "At least give it a try, all right?"

"All right," Emika said.

"Well, I better go." Rosa started back down the steps to the driveway. "See you at the Vancouver tournament!"

"Can't wait! See you then," Emika said.

Rosa paused mid-step and turned back to Emika. "You'll do great, you know. You and Maram."

Emika gave a small shrug.

"You're both good at different things," Rosa said. "You two are like peanut butter and chocolate. My favourite kind of candy bar."

Emika waved good-bye as Rosa and her dad drove away. Then she closed the door and ripped open the present. It was a small hardcover book called *Wolfpack*. Emika didn't even open the book to look inside. She tossed it onto the small table in the hallway. Unless it was going to teach her how to stop Maram from being cold and bossy, she had no interest in reading it. Even if it came from Rosa.

4 Coin TOSS

The next Saturday afternoon the Wolves had a game against the Sooke Thunder. Emika took her time walking with Jabira to the field. Since leaving her house, Emika's stomach had been fluttering at the thought of leading the team. She told herself she shouldn't be nervous. But her mind had gone blank. She couldn't remember a single thing that a captain was supposed to do.

Jabira pulled a small wagon loaded with the team's oranges, water bottles and first-aid kit. "What's up with you today? You're walking slower than I am."

Emika took a deep breath. For some reason, she was embarrassed to admit that she wasn't feeling confident. "Lots to think about. Going over captain things."

"Won't be easy filling Rosa's shoes," Jabira said. "She did a lot as captain."

Emika tried to sound casual. "Maybe we should list some of those things. You know, as a way to honour her legacy."

They walked another block before Jabira offered an idea. "For one thing, Rosa always led the pre-game warm-up. You know the warm-up routine. That part is easy."

Easy, Emika thought. *Unless a certain someone tries to take over.*

"Then there's getting the team roster to the referee." Jabira smirked at Emika. "You can deliver a piece of paper, can't you?"

"That part sounds tricky," Emika joked. "But . . . two captains. Are we supposed to carry a piece of paper together?"

"I'm sure you can take turns," Jabira said.

They turned the corner and headed up a steep hill. Emika helped Jabira pull the wagon over the sidewalk curb.

"Oh, and the coin toss," Jabira said. "To choose side or ball possession."

Emika snorted. "Great. I'll choose heads, Maram will choose tails and the game will never get started."

The wagon handle slipped from Jabira's hand and clanged on the concrete. Emika swooped down to pick it up. Seeing Jabira work so hard to get her fingers back around the handle made Emika feel silly for being so worried.

"Rosa was also responsible for talking to the referee if we had a question about a foul," Jabira said.

Emika remembered the season before when Nina

had sprained her ankle. They had been playing the same team they were playing today, the Sooke Thunder, and a Thunder player had checked Nina with a slide tackle. There had been no penalty called on the play, even though Nina had to be carried off the field. Rosa had calmly explained their side to the referee.

"She slid into our player, cleats first," Rosa had said. "She didn't touch the ball at all. Why wasn't a penalty called?"

Rosa had not won that discussion with the referee, but the Wolves got a couple of free kicks called their way after that.

"And most importantly," Jabira said as they neared the field, "Rosa got the team pumped up. Before the game, during the game and after the game."

Nobody can do that like Rosa, Emika thought with a sigh. Rosa could make everybody determined to win with just a few words.

When they arrived at the field, the Sooke Thunder were already stretching together as a team. All the Wolves players sat on the sidelines lacing up their cleats and putting on their shin pads.

Emika grew tense as she counted her teammates. Everyone had arrived before her.

"Also, Rosa was always the first one to show up for the games." Jabira flashed Emika a teasing smile.

Emika's stomach sank. Her first game as a captain was not off to a good start.

As Coach Garcia talked to the team, Emika hurried out of her track pants. Everyone else was nearly ready. That meant the team would start the warm-up before Emika had her cleats tied up. And that meant Maram would lead the warm-up without her.

"Going to be a tough one today," Coach Garcia said. "The Thunder has a strong defence and an even stronger midfield. We need to keep our passes short and quick. And move to the ball, don't wait for it to come to you. Now go warm up and get ready to play."

Without a word, Maram ran out onto the field. For a moment, the team stood motionless on the sidelines.

"Are we supposed to head out there?" Kelly asked Emika.

Emika hesitated by focusing intensely on pulling her long soccer socks over her shin pads. If she stalled long enough, Maram couldn't take over the warm-up all by herself.

Jusdeep spoiled the plan. "Let's go, Wolves. Maram's starting the warm-up."

The teammates walked back and forth across the field, dropping down into lunges every few steps. Emika sat on her duffel bag next to Jabira and pulled on her soccer cleats. She laced them up, then headed onto the field to join her team, flustered at entering the warm-up so late. To make up for it, Emika tried to get the team excited for the game.

"This game is ours, Wolves!" Emika called out as they ran side shuffles. Her rally cry didn't have Rosa's pizzazz, but at least it was something.

Maram moved the team onto stretches.

As Emika stretched, she tried to get into game mode by picturing herself playing. One time she had read an article about how visualizing your sports moves was as good as actual practice. She tried to see herself beating the defenders with fast dekes. She tried to picture her corner kicks sailing high and far into the front of the goal. It wasn't working. The thought that she had been late for warm-up kept creeping into her brain.

When the team came off the field, Coach Garcia held out a clipboard to both Maram and Emika. "Run the roster sheet over to the referee."

Maram hopped to it right away. She took the piece of paper off the clipboard and ran off with the roster, leaving Emika behind.

Nice try, thought Emika. *I'm not going to let you take over everything.*

Emika sprinted out to the middle of the field to join Maram. The referee and the Sooke captain joined them. Maram handed the referee the team roster.

The referee held a coin in her open palm. "Heads or tails, Wolves?"

"Heads," Emika said quickly.

The coin flipped into the air. The referee caught it and smacked it onto the back of her hand. "Heads," she said. "Do you want possession of ball or choice of side?"

Emika blurted out, "Possession of ball!"

The referee shook hands with the captains. "Wolves kick off first."

Maram stared hard at Emika. "Should've chosen side, not possession. Now we'll be staring straight at the sun for the whole first half."

"So? What's the big deal?" Emika contested. "They'll be staring at it for the whole second half."

"No, they won't." Maram pointed at the line of tall cedars at the far end of the field. "The sun will be behind the trees by then."

Emika looked at the position of the sun, realizing her mistake. Maram was right. But there was no way Emika was going to admit it.

5 CORNERED

The Wolves lined up for the kick-off. The sun shone brightly in their eyes. The entire forward line shielded their faces from the glare. Except Emika. She squinted and pretended it didn't bother her, even though her eyes watered. But it was almost impossible to see up the field.

The play started with Kelly dribbling up the centre. Emika exploded along the wing but she couldn't lose her check. The Thunder midfielders were speedy.

"Emika!" Kelly kicked the ball up the wing.

The midfielder checking Emika took the ball and sent a short pass to another Thunder player. The team's one-touch passes were lightning fast and perfectly on target. After six short passes up the middle of the field, one of the Thunder forwards drilled the ball at the goal.

"You got this, Jusdeep!" Emika yelled from up the field.

But Jusdeep didn't move. She just stood in net like a statue as the ball whizzed past her and into the goal.

The Thunder cheered.

At first, Emika was puzzled. What was Jusdeep thinking? Why didn't she try?

Emika smacked her forehead. Of course, Jusdeep couldn't see any better than the rest of the players. She had been completely blinded by the sun.

All because I picked the wrong thing at coin toss, Emika thought. It was her fault that the Thunder scored such an early goal. Had even one minute passed since opening kick-off? What kind of captain made decisions like that?

Meanwhile the Thunder team gathered at the top of the eighteen-yard box. They huddled close together with their arms wrapped around each other. Their captain led them in a short cheer. They stomped their feet in unison.

"Who are we?"

"THUNDER!"

"Who are we?"

"THUNDER!"

Emika looked around the field at the Wolves. Some walked back to their positions, kicking at the grass. Some tilted their heads skyward, their hands on their hips in what looked like defeat. After a six-game winning streak, the Wolves weren't used to being scored on so quickly. Emika had to think of something to pick them up. But what?

She checked her teammates' faces, trying to get a sense of how they were feeling. Something that might help her figure out what to say. That's when she noticed Nina. Normally, Nina was a constant buzz of energy. But now she walked slowly and her face looked troubled.

As the referee jogged the ball up the field to the centre line, Emika quickly made her way over to Nina. "Something's wrong, I can tell," Emika said. "Is it the goal? We'll get it back."

Nina looked over at one of the Thunder defenders. "Last time we played this team, I sprained my ankle. What if it's a rough game again? I couldn't play soccer for two weeks after that."

Emika rested her hand on Nina's shoulder. "Then you just take it easy. No one's going to blame you if you back off the play a little. Do whatever feels right for you."

Nina's face lit up. "Okay. Thanks, Emika."

"Quick, bring it in, forwards!" Maram called. She stood by herself at centre, ready to kick off. She jumped up and down, looking eager to play.

Once the forwards had gathered, Maram said, "Remember. Short passes. Nothing long. Kelly, it might have been a good pass but I'm betting you couldn't really see Emika. Not with that sun in our eyes."

Emika squeezed her hands into fists. *I get it*, she thought. *I made the wrong decision. You don't have to rub it in my face.*

"I can't make short passes if the wingers are too far up the field," Kelly said.

"Wingers should be hanging back," Maram said.

Emika reminded Maram, "You're a winger, too."

"Not anymore. I'm taking centre forward. Nina, you take my winger spot."

Now Maram was trying to take over Rosa's old position? What next?

Emika was certain that Nina, who had started the game at centre forward, would stand up to Maram. But Nina nodded.

"Makes sense," Nina said.

During the next few plays, the Wolves midfielders started to work the ball around using short, crisp passes. They talked to each other, too. They called for the passes, and talked when they were moving to the ball. They warned each other when a Thunder player was coming to check them from behind. It kept the speedy Thunder players on their toes.

But whenever the Wolves midfielders tried to pass it up to the forward line, the forwards lost the ball to the Thunder. Sometimes they tried to dribble it too far on their own. Other times they made bad passes.

"Come on, forwards!" Kelly shouted. "Start talking to each other!"

By the second half, the score was still 1–0 for the Thunder.

With the sun no longer in her eyes, Emika was

ready to push for a tie at least. After a tough battle for the ball, Kelly belted a long ball up the field. Emika sprinted up the wing, angling toward the net as Maram chased the ball up the middle. By the time Maram caught up to the ball, she had an open path in front of her. Just inside the eighteen-yard box, Maram launched a powerful shot at the goal.

The Thunder goalkeeper dived past the post and punched the ball out of bounds.

The Wolves' offence hurried to set up for the corner kick.

"Let's tie it up here, Wolves!" Emika called out.

Pumped with the chance to set up a goal, Emika hurried to get the ball for the corner kick. She rolled the ball with her fingertips until it settled on the grass next to the corner flag just the way she wanted it. To her surprise, Emika stood upright to see Maram in front of her.

"I'm taking the corner kick," Maram said.

Emika scrunched her eyebrows. "But I always take the corner kicks."

"I'm taking it this time," Maram said. "You need to be next to the post."

"Players!" the referee called. "Let's get the game going."

Bending over, Maram moved the ball a few inches over.

Emika huffed loudly. "Who put you in charge?"

"Coach Garcia. And Rosa," Maram said.

"They made me captain, too," Emika argued.

"Are you two planning to go head to head like this all game?" asked the referee.

Maram pointed Emika at the goal. "I need you next to the post ready for another header. Like at practice."

"Last warning, Wolves," said the referee. "Or my yellow card is coming out."

Emika looked at the other players lined up in front of the goal. Several of them stood with their hands on their hips, waiting.

"Are we going to play or what?" Kelly called out.

Fed up, Emika took a deep breath and hurried to the goal area. As soon as Emika was positioned next to the post, Maram raised her arm to signal she was about to kick. With a skip and a hop, she launched the ball into the air.

Emika watched it fly toward her. It had a perfect banana curve on it, just like the one at practice. She got set for another header.

But the goalie was set, too. She jumped sideways, stretching her arm toward the crossbar. She couldn't reach it. Neither could Emika.

Maram's kick curved right over Emika's head and into the top corner of the goal.

The referee blew the whistle.

"Wow!" exclaimed one of the Thunder players next to Emika. "I've never seen anyone score on a corner kick like that."

"I've never seen two captains argue like that," said the Thunder goalkeeper.

Several players laughed.

Emika felt her cheeks burn with embarrassment. Quickly she headed back to the centre line to get out of earshot. She didn't want to be around to hear any more.

"If someone on our team could shoot like that," another one of them said, her voice fading as Emika jogged away, "I sure wouldn't argue about who gets to take the corner kick."

6 Cups and POTS

The game ended in a 1–1 tie. But the Wolves acted like they'd lost 10–0. That's how it seemed to Emika, anyhow. All her teammates were far away in their thoughts. Not just from her. From each other, too. It felt like when a string of beads breaks and all the beads scatter in different directions.

As the Wolves quietly changed out of their cleats, Coach Garcia pulled Maram and Emika aside.

Good. Emika crossed her arms in satisfaction. *Now Coach Garcia will tell Maram that she shouldn't have insisted on taking the corner kick. Even if she had scored.*

But Coach Garcia didn't mention the corner kick at all. Or the argument. "On Tuesday," Coach Garcia said, "you two will run the practice. Together."

Emika's arms dropped to her sides. *Together?*

"Sounds good, Coach," Maram said.

Coach Garcia glanced at Emika. "Sound good to you, too?"

Emika hesitated for a moment. No one understood

what it was like for Emika to have to deal with Maram. Why couldn't Coach Garcia and the rest of the team see what Maram was truly like? Why was no one else upset by how bossy she was?

Coach Garcia raised her eyebrows in question.

Emika said, "Sounds good, Coach."

Coach Garcia walked away, leaving the two girls on the sideline. Around them, their teammates continued to unzip and zip their duffel bags, change into their shoes and pull on their track pants. One by one, they started to leave the field.

"See you on Tuesday, Nina," Emika said.

Nina gave Emika a half-hearted nod as she walked toward the parking lot.

"Good job in net, Jusdeep," Maram said.

"Nice goal, Maram," Jusdeep said, but her voice was small and flat.

Then Jabira walked past Emika and Maram, pulling her wagon.

"See you later, Jabira," Emika called out.

Jabira lifted her hand and waved over her shoulder.

For a few moments, Emika watched her teammates wander off in different directions. She tugged her track pants out of her bag and said, "This was a bad idea."

Maram sat on the grass and struggled with a knot in her laces.

Emika undid the Velcro straps on her shin pads.

"We should tell Coach Garcia that we don't want to be captains."

"Speak for yourself. I want to be a captain," said Maram.

Emika pulled off her other shin pad. "But you know it's not going to work out. You and me being captains together."

Maram looked up. There was something about Maram's face that always froze Emika for a second. Maybe it was because she never smiled. Or maybe it was because she seemed to have no expression at all. Her mouth reminded Emika of a ruler. Always straight, never bending.

"I'm happy that Rosa picked me," Maram said.

Emika had never thought about Maram being happy about anything. But the mention of Rosa struck a chord in Emika. If there was one thing Emika and Maram had in common, it was their old captain. Everyone loved Rosa. Even ruler-faced Maram.

"I'm happy that Rosa picked me, too," Emika said. "But I don't think Rosa would be happy to know that you're trying to take over everything."

"I'm not taking over everything," said Maram. "I'm being a leader."

Emika laughed. "By bossing everybody around? By taking my corner kicks?"

"Sometimes you have to demand the ball," Maram shrugged.

Cups and Pots

Emika strained to get her cleat off. "Why? Because you think you're better than everybody else?"

"Because I believe in myself. And I was right. I scored."

Emika rose to her feet and stood on the grass, cleats on one foot and a sock on the other foot. "You act like you're too good for everyone else. You act like you're too good for me. You even act like you're too good for your own sister."

Maram also rose to her feet. Her eyes widened with what looked like anger. It was the most expression Emika had ever seen on Maram's face and it took her by surprise.

Maram snatched her duffel bag off the ground and stormed off in her socks, her running shoes still clutched in her other hand.

★ ★ ★

At home that evening, Emika headed downstairs to the basement. Kaito sat at his pottery wheel. He had been busy lately getting ready for a big art show. His foot pumped a pedal that made the small wheel turn. In the middle of the wheel was a piece of clay. Kaito shaped the spinning clay with his thumbs.

Emika sank into a big armchair and Sinclair flopped onto her feet. When she had received the golden retriever, her parents had already named him after Emika's favourite soccer player, Christine Sinclair.

"You'll never believe what's happened to our soccer team," Emika told Kaito as she stroked Sinclair's head.

Kaito kept working on the clay. He was concentrating, but Emika knew he was listening. He always listened to her.

"Coach Garcia and Rosa appointed Maram and me as co-captains."

"That's a big honour," Kaito said.

"But . . . *Maram*," Emika said. "We don't like each other. Not even a little."

"How come?" Kaito stopped the pottery wheel.

"I don't know why she doesn't like me. I never did anything to her."

"Why don't you like her?" Kaito dipped his fingertips in some water.

"She bosses everybody around, for one thing."

"Like how?" Kaito asked.

"She tells people what plays to do and where to stand," Emika replied.

"Didn't Rosa do that, too?" Kaito asked, spinning the wheel again.

Emika thought about it. "Yeah, but she did it differently."

"Oh," Kaito said, raising his eyebrows.

"She's just so cold to me. And to Jabira. She never talks to Jabira at soccer."

The piece of clay was starting to take shape. Maybe a pot for a tiny seedling of a houseplant or a Japanese cup for tea. Kaito was in grade twelve and had won many awards for art at his high school.

"Have you ever tried to get to know Maram?" Kaito asked.

Emika groaned.

Kaito laughed. "It's just . . . maybe you're wrong about her."

"I'm not wrong," said Emika.

Kaito held his hands on either side of his creation. "Ta-da!"

"I love it." Emika smiled.

"Do you know what it is?" Kaito asked.

"A teacup?"

"Right. It's a teacup."

The shelves along the basement wall were lined with pots and cups and small clay monsters. Some were painted. Some were left plain. In the summer, Kaito sold his pottery at a booth near the harbourfront.

"But you only know that because you know that Japanese teacups don't have handles," Kaito said. "People who don't know that would have guessed it's a small pot. It all depends on what you know about a thing. Sometimes a person thinks a thing is a pot, but it's not a pot. It's something else. And sometimes a person thinks a thing is a cup, but it's not a cup. It's something else."

★ ★ ★

Before bed, Emika got out some paper and drew a soccer field on it. She went to her computer and searched for soccer drills. She copied them on the paper. There was no way she was going to let Maram take over practice like she had taken over the warm-up. After that corner kick, Emika wanted to show the others that she could take charge, too.

Before shutting off the computer, Emika checked the weather forecast. She checked every night to see what the weather would be like for their next game day.

Sunny, with light clouds.

At least the weather was looking up.

7 The PRACTICE

Emika arrived early to practice on Tuesday. In her pocket she carried the folded-up piece of paper with her drills mapped out. She didn't think she would remember how the drills played out without the paper.

Coach Garcia stood on the sidelines. "Only here to supervise," she told Emika and Maram. "Other than that, the whole show is up to you two today."

Maram sprinted onto the field without a word, expecting that the rest of the team would follow.

This time, however, Emika wasn't going to let her take charge that easily. Emika sprinted past Maram. She stood at the top of the eighteen-yard box, facing her team. Before Maram had a chance to say anything, Emika shouted, "High knees to the centre line and back!"

All the Wolves players took a few quick steps, jumping their knees up high.

"No, stop!" Maram shouted. "Back to the line!"

The players stopped and walked back to the goal line.

Erika glared at Maram, then turned to her team and repeated, "High knees to the centre line!"

Kelly and Jusdeep looked puzzled. After hesitating for a moment, they started the high knees exercise again.

Maram raised her hand. "Stop! Back to the line."

"What do you think you're doing?" Emika asked.

"Since when do we start a warm-up with high knees?" Maram asked. "Someone is going to get injured. Okay, Wolves! Let's start with a slow jog to the centre line and back, followed by a light side shuffle."

Emika frowned. Maram was right. What was she thinking, starting off a warm-up like that? At least she had her drills in her pocket.

While Maram joined the team in the warm-up, Emika grabbed orange cones and the bag of soccer balls from the sidelines and took them to the other end of the soccer field. She set one cone about twenty-five feet away from the goal. Then she dumped the balls out onto the goal line.

When the team had finished stretching, Emika called them down to her end of the soccer field. "We're going to work on our one-on-one skills," she explained. "Defenders line up down at the goal line here. Forwards and midfielders line up at the cone. Jusdeep, we need you in net. Once the defender passes the ball out to the cone, it's one-on-one to the goal."

Emika looked at Maram, who was shaking her head.

Suddenly Emika felt a prickle of doubt, but she pushed on anyway.

Ayana Ferguson, a defender, passed the ball out to Kelly, who dribbled the ball back and forth between her feet as she approached the goal. Jusdeep crouched low, her arms spread out wide and her big goalie gloves ready for the shot. Ayana raced to Kelly and poked at the ball with her feet. But Kelly was quick and burst past her with an explosive deke. The shot moved hard along the ground. Jusdeep dived and stopped the ball with her outstretched hands.

The whole team cheered. "Great save, Jusdeep!"

As the next pair of players got ready for the drill, Emika said to Jusdeep, "You sure know how to read a shot, Jusdeep."

Jusdeep smiled. "Thanks, Emika."

Emika added, "Glad you're on our team."

After two more plays, Maram marched into the centre of everybody, with both hands in the air. "Okay, time to move on to the next drill."

"Already?" Kelly asked. "We've only done this one for a few minutes."

"But we're a strong team one-on-one," Maram said. "There are other things we need to practice more."

Emika put her hands on her hips. "Says who?"

Behind her, Jusdeep whispered to Nina. "Here we go again. Another argument."

"Fine, we'll move on to the next drill," Emika said. But she refused to help Maram rearrange the cones.

"Four corners," Maram said. "To help us work on our short-pass game." Maram demonstrated how the aim of the drill was to pass to a teammate who was inside one of the smaller corner squares, marked by the cones.

"One point to each team that does it."

She tossed practice jerseys to the players, dividing them into a red team and a blue team.

Emika remembered this drill from her computer search. She wished she had thought of using it instead of Maram leading it.

As the drill went on, the Wolves players moved the ball around well. Once in a while, somebody would stand in one of the four corners to receive a pass.

"Point for Team Red!" Maram shouted.

"Wait!" Emika said.

Everybody stopped.

"What now?" Kelly grumbled.

"You're not doing it right," Emika said.

"Yes, they are," Maram insisted.

"No, they're not."

Nina groaned. "How are we supposed to do it, then?"

Emika detected a hint of sarcasm in Nina's voice, but she ignored it. "The person receiving the pass in the little squares isn't supposed to just stand there and wait.

They're supposed to be running into the square when they get the pass."

"Sure, if you're doing the advanced version," said Maram. "But this is a good start. We'll build up to that at another practice."

"I just think we should do it the right way from the start," said Emika.

Kelly pointed at Maram. "I agree with Maram. Let's start with the simple version and get good at that first."

Emika pursed her lips. Now Kelly was agreeing with Maram?

"Fine," Emika said. "Run the drill however you want."

Emika walked off to the sidelines. She squirted water into her mouth even though she hadn't done any exercising with the team.

"Not much of a wolf pack out there," said Jabira. She was taking inventory of the first-aid kit. "More like a couple of lone wolves."

Emika didn't say a word. It was already getting hard — almost impossible — to believe in Rosa's choice, no matter how much Emika wanted to trust Rosa like she'd said she would.

At the end of practice, Coach Garcia reminded the team that the Vancouver tournament was soon.

"Two weeks. We need to raise a little more money for it," Coach Garcia said. "I'll leave it up to our two captains to decide together what type of fundraising we'll do."

A few players groaned.

"Can't you decide for us, Coach?" Jusdeep asked.

"We'll never get it done if those two have to decide," somebody else mumbled.

"A car wash," Maram said. "At the gas station on Nickel Street during rush hour next week. We'll make lots of money. Guaranteed."

"That's a great idea," Ayana said. "We could make signs at my house on Sunday."

"It's a terrible idea," said Emika. "It's supposed to rain all week. Nobody gets their car washed in the rain."

"Guess we should watch the weather report," said Coach Garcia, "and decide another day."

But Emika knew the weather report would prove her wrong. She knew it was supposed to be sunny with light clouds all week. Maram was going to get her way again.

★ ★ ★

As Emika flopped into bed that night, she thought about how badly soccer practice had gone. She wondered what she should do. It seemed like the team was siding with Maram more and more. She had to show the team that she was as good a captain as Maram. But how?

Especially when Maram kept taking over everything. Emika needed to find a way to win the team over.

An idea popped into her head. She jumped out of bed and turned on her computer.

In the top corner of the screen was a little window. A chat group for the Wolves players. The last messages were sad good-byes to Rosa from all her teammates. Emika scrolled up to see the older messages from a few weeks ago. Before and after every game, Rosa always sent a positive note to each player on the team. It put everybody in good spirits. It lifted the whole team up.

Emika closed the group window. Instead, she messaged the players one at a time.

Pizza and movies Friday night. Six. My house.

8 Secret MEETING

On Friday, Emika got bowls of popcorn and chips ready. She had spent her babysitting money on snacks and had set aside another thirty dollars for pizza. Convincing her teammates that she was the best leader with the best ideas was totally worth spending her savings.

Kelly was the first to arrive, on her bike. Then Ayana and Jusdeep were dropped off by Ayana's dad. Nina, Wendy and Gabrielle took the bus together.

"When's the rest of the team getting here?" Kelly asked, tossing a piece of popcorn into her mouth.

"This is it, just you six," said Emika.

"Oh, I thought this was a team night," Ayana said.

"Sort of, but not really," said Emika. "Some of the team couldn't come. But also, it's not really a team thing. Just pizza and movies."

"What are we watching? Something scary?" Jusdeep grinned.

Emika set the chip bowls on the coffee table. "All the movies are over there on the little shelves beside the TV."

The girls sat on the floor next to the coffee table and dug into the snacks.

Jusdeep turned around with a DVD in her hand. "*Bend It Like Beckham!*"

Emika smiled. The soccer movie about a women's team was one of Emika's favourites. She'd seen it more than thirty times and she was willing to watch it thirty more.

"I wish Jabira was here," Kelly said. "She loves this movie. She recites every single word of it. It drives me nuts, but it's kind of funny."

Emika felt guilty for not inviting Jabira. But if Jabira had come, she might have figured out that Emika had invited everyone except Maram.

"Too bad," Emika nodded.

As Jusdeep turned on the DVD player and slid the movie inside, Nina asked, "What does it mean to bend it like Beckham?"

Kelly explained, "It's how the great soccer player, David Beckham, could curl the ball around a wall of defenders when he took a free kick."

Ayana agreed. "Just like how Maram curled the ball into the net from the corner kick. That was unreal."

"I've been practising that kick with my mom since I saw Maram do it," Kelly said.

"Yeah, it was amazing," said Emika. "But what was with her taking over practice on Tuesday? And her idea about the car wash?"

"I thought it was a great idea," shrugged Jusdeep. "My brother's field hockey team did a car wash. People give lots of tips at those things."

"But who wants to get all cold and wet?" Emika argued.

Ayana laughed. "We get cold and wet almost every soccer game."

"You just don't like the idea because . . ." Jusdeep stopped.

The girls looked at each other awkwardly. Kelly stuffed a handful of chips into her mouth.

"Just say it. Because it came from Maram," Nina finished Jusdeep's thought.

Emika frowned. "That's not why."

Nina raised her eyebrows at Emika.

"What have you two got against each other, anyway?" Ayana asked.

Emika was growing tired of people asking her that question. First Kelly. Then Kaito. Now Ayana.

"Don't you think she comes across as kind of strict?" Emika asked.

"A little, I guess," said Kelly. "She can be pretty intense at times."

"Only because she loves soccer so much," said Ayana.

Emika rolled her eyes and wondered, *if she loves soccer, how come she won't play with her own sister?*

About five minutes into the movie, Emika got up to get more juice.

"Want us to pause it?" Jusdeep asked.

Emika shook her head. "I know this movie inside-out."

Alone in the kitchen, Emika felt disappointed. The evening was not going as planned. First of all, only six teammates had been able to come over. And now she needed to find a way to convince the ones who were here to not follow Maram's lead or her ideas. She needed to convince them that she had better ideas. The problem was that Emika hadn't come up with a single idea for fundraising. They'd already sold chocolate almonds earlier in the year. And they'd done two bottle drives.

When she went back to the living room, the girls were erupting into laughter at the movie. Just as Emika sat down, the doorbell rang.

"Pizza! I'm starving," Nina said.

Grabbing her money from the shelf, Emika ran down the stairs to the front door and flung it open. But it wasn't the pizza delivery person.

Emika's mouth dropped. "Jabira. Hi."

Jabira stood there with her soccer ball under her arm.

"Want to hit the park?" she asked.

"Oh . . ." Emika didn't know what to say.

"We can practise our shooting." Jabira smiled.

"Can't today," Emika said. "My mom said I have to do chores."

Jabira scrunched her eyebrows. "On a Friday night?"

From upstairs, the girls' laughter rang out.

One of the girls exclaimed, "I love this part!"

"That sounds like Kelly," Jabira said.

"Play that part over again!" That was Nina's voice.

Jabira looked at Emika. "Is the team here?"

"No, just a few players," Emika said.

"Oh," Jabira said.

Emika looked down at the doormat.

"Is Maram here, too?" Jabira asked.

Emika flashed Jabira a look of confusion. Jabira knew better than to think Maram would ever be at Emika's house.

Jabira said, "Because if it's a team thing, Maram should be here, too."

Why was Jabira so protective of her sister all of sudden?

"Is she here, Emika?" Jabira pressed.

Emika shook her head.

Jabira gave Emika a long look. Because of her cerebral palsy, sometimes the muscles in Jabira's face worked overtime. So many people found it hard to know how Jabira was feeling from her facial expression. But Emika had been friends with Jabira long enough to tell when she was upset.

"Hope you finish your *chores* soon," Jabira said.

Jabira made her way back down the front steps without another word. Just then, the pizza delivery person pulled into the driveway. Jabira looked at the pizza logo on the side of the car and shook her head.

Suddenly, Emika wasn't hungry.

9 Team SPIRIT

The next day, the Wolves played against the Langford Waves. Emika waited on her front steps to walk with Jabira to the field. As she listened for the sound of Jabira's wagon wheels scraping along the sidewalk, Emika thought about what she should do. She had to patch things up with Jabira after the pizza party. But how? What exactly was the big deal? It wasn't like the whole team had been there . . .

Only because the others couldn't make it, she admitted to herself. On top of that, she had lied to Jabira about having chores to do.

Emika's stomach felt uneasy. What if Jabira found out that Emika had invited everyone except her and Maram?

Finally, Emika left for the field on her own. She couldn't risk being late for the warm-up again.

At the field, Emika spotted Jabira chatting with Coach Garcia. Maram and a few other Wolves players juggled soccer balls along the sidelines. Emika nodded hello to Jabira. Jabira smiled.

A feeling of relief washed over Emika. *Maybe she's not even upset*, she thought. *But then why didn't she stop by my house? We always walk to the games together.*

From the start, it looked as though the Waves were going to dominate the game.

After the kick-off, Maram passed the ball back to Kelly. Kelly tried to blast the ball over to Ayana but a Waves player intercepted it and made a pass up the wing. Nina chased after the forward dribbling down the field. But then Nina tripped and tumbled onto the ground. The Waves forward cut in toward the net and took a shot.

Jusdeep made the save, cradling the ball against her stomach with both arms. She punted it back up the field.

Emika dug her cleats into the grass and trapped the ball with her thigh. She turned and spotted Ayana coming up the middle. Emika sent a long pass, hoping Ayana would be able to chase it down. Before Ayana could reach it, one of the Waves defenders belted the ball back down the field to the same winger who had just shot on the Wolves' goal.

This time, the winger managed to dribble closer into the goal area. Emika watched the Wolves defenders run back to protect the net. She cringed. They were practically bumping into Jusdeep, who craned her head from side to side to get a clear view of the ball.

The shot went straight into the top corner of the Wolves' goal.

As the Waves celebrated their goal, Maram came up behind Emika.

"Long passes won't work against this team," Maram said. "We're working on our short game, remember?"

"The short game hasn't been working either," Emika said.

"It will, if you give it a chance," Maram said.

Emika knew Maram was right. At the last game, the midfielders had ended up controlling the play with their quick, short passes. And Maram had been right about the corner kick, too. In fact, Maram had been right about everything. Emika's coin toss decision. The warm-up at practice. The one-on-one drills that Emika ran.

Couldn't I be right about something, Emika thought. *Even just once?*

The referee blew her whistle. Maram kicked off, making a short pass to Emika. Emika nudged the ball past a Waves player and immediately crossed the ball far ahead to the opposite side where Ayana was supposed to be. It rolled out of bounds.

Maram narrowed her eyes at Emika. "Did you blow that pass on purpose?"

"You seriously think I'd do that?" Emika asked.

Kelly sighed. "Would you two stop it? You're going to wreck the whole game again."

Meanwhile, the Waves player had thrown the ball in from out of bounds. Their star winger again took the ball up the sidelines. She crossed it to the middle of the eighteen-yard box. One of the Waves players sprinted toward the goal and got a toe on the ball, putting it past Jusdeep, who slid feet-first into the player.

It was 2–0 Waves.

"See? Two long passes. Two goals," Emika pointed out. She mumbled this under her breath so that only Maram could hear.

"Different teams have different strengths and weaknesses," Maram said. "Just like different people do."

The rest of the first half didn't go any better. None of the passes the Wolves tried seemed to be clicking. So Emika kept trying to beat the Waves players on her own. Maram, too, tried to deke her way up the field. But the Waves defenders shut them both down.

At half-time, Coach Garcia asked, "What's going on out there, Wolves? It's one thing to be losing. But no one looks like they're having any fun."

Emika looked around at her teammates. Not one of them smiled. Not one of them goofed around like they always did during half-time. Coach Garcia was right. No one was having any fun.

Who can have any fun with Maram on the field? Emika thought. *She is always so serious about everything.*

The game got even worse for the Wolves in the second half. All of the Wolves players seemed to have given up passing altogether. Instead, it was every player for herself. Even Nina and Kelly, two of their best passers, tried to get through the Waves' defensive line on their own.

Finally, the game ended in a 2–0 victory for the Langford Waves.

Emika studied the body language of her teammates as they gathered around Coach Garcia. Heads hung low. Shoulders slumped. There was just no energy in the team.

"Where has your team spirit gone?" Coach Garcia asked.

At first no one said a thing.

Then Maram piped up. "We'll get it back, Coach. Failure is our fuel."

Emika winced. *That's what Rosa said after I missed those corner kicks at practice.*

"Can we get our team spirit back before the Vancouver tournament?" Jusdeep asked. "Be nice if Rosa didn't see us like this."

Kelly agreed. "It would be embarrassing."

"I know what will bring the team together," Maram said. "The car wash. My dad has set up the whole thing. Be at the Nickel Street gas station this Monday at four-thirty."

"Wait," Emika protested. "We were supposed to decide together."

"We did decide," Maram said. "I asked everyone on our team chat group."

For a moment Emika felt betrayed. The team had decided something without her. Then she remembered that she'd closed the chat group window on her computer and hadn't checked it since.

"You know, our team chat group?" Maram said. "The team chat group you're supposed to use to ask the *whole* team stuff?"

Emika flashed a look at Jabira. When Jabira's cheeks flushed, Emika knew for certain that Jabira had told her sister about Emika's pizza party. Emika wanted to be upset with Jabira but she couldn't, for one simple reason.

Emika knew she had made a mistake.

Emika took the long way home after the game. At a street corner near the field, she overheard Ayana and Nina talking. They were waiting for Nina's mom at her car. Just as Emika was about to call out to them, Ayana grumbled something to Nina about a "captain."

Emika stopped in front of a pickup truck that was parked two cars away from Ayana and Nina. She hid next to the front fender.

"I wish Coach Garcia had let us vote for captain," Ayana said.

"What was she thinking, appointing those two?" Nina asked.

"Maybe Coach can't hear how they argue on the field," Ayana said. "I bet if we explained what's going on, she would let us vote for a captain."

Emika's heart sank. Was it Emika they had a problem with, or was it Maram?

Or is it both of us? she wondered.

10 FAILURE

The second Emika got home, she opened the team chat group to check out the discussion about the car wash. Sure enough, everyone on the team seemed to love about the idea. Emika was the only one who hadn't answered at all.

Just then, her computer went *ding!* with an incoming message. It was from Gabrielle Sabatini, their best defender.

Wolves, I'm sorry to say this, but I'm thinking of quitting the team.

Emika stared at the message, trying to make sense of it. Some dots appeared at the bottom of the chat group, signalling that someone was typing a message. Emika waited, hoping that one of the Wolves was going to tell Gabrielle not to quit.

I can understand that.

It was Kelly.

Emika felt a heaviness in her belly. What did Kelly mean by that? What did she "understand"?

Someone else started typing. The next thing Emika knew, she was watching the team unravel before her eyes.

I was thinking the same thing.
About quitting?
Yeah.
Me too.
Same here.
I hate to say it. But it's just not fun anymore.

Emika took note of who was in the chat. Ayana, Nina and Jusdeep had joined the conversation. Emika waited for ten minutes to see if anybody else was going to say anything. There was nothing more.

But it was plenty. Emika knew she had to do something drastic. At least, she had to do something different. She remembered Jabira and the bendable straws that helped her to overcome the tremors in her hands. "Would you trust these hands to not toss your bubble tea everywhere?" Jabira had asked her. "I don't. So I learn to do things differently."

Unlike Jabira, Emika had no idea how to do things differently. But she had to figure it out, and soon. She had no choice. The fate of the Wolves depended on it.

Failure

★ ★ ★

Emika sat at the kitchen table, eating a grilled cheese sandwich. Even a bad soccer game made her hungry, though every chew took a lot of sad effort. She broke off a chunk and fed it to Sinclair under the table.

"What's up with you?" Kaito asked as he walked into the kitchen and opened the fridge door. His apron was coated in splotches of wet clay. "You look like one of my pots when they collapse into a folded lump on my pottery wheel."

Emika glanced up at her brother but didn't say a word.

Kaito poured himself a glass of milk. "Let me guess. The co-captain thing is going as bad as you expected."

Emika swallowed her bite. "I thought the problem would be Maram. But now I'm not so sure. Maybe I'm not meant to be a captain."

"I don't think that's true." Kaito squeezed chocolate syrup into his milk and stirred it with a spoon.

"When Rosa was captain, everyone had fun. We worked as a team. Even Maram and I worked together." Emika dropped the half-eaten sandwich onto her plate. "A bunch of the players are thinking of quitting."

"How come?" Kaito wiped a milk moustache from his lips.

Emika pointed to a spot he'd missed. "Rosa's gone. That's how come."

His eyes widened. "Was she a wizard or something? Did she cast a spell on the team?"

Emika knew Kaito was joking. But in a way, it *did* feel like Rosa was able to cast a spell on the team. "She just had a special way of leading us."

"Some people are naturals," Kaito nodded. "But the rest of us mere mortals have to learn how to lead."

"I keep making the wrong decisions. I feel like a failure." Emika shook her head with a sigh. "How am I supposed to learn? Go to captain school?"

"You can learn from captains like Rosa." Kaito looked down at Sinclair, who started wagging his tail at the attention. "From captains like Christine Sinclair. From captains like Abby Wambach. And you stick with it no matter what. You use failure as your fuel."

"What does everybody keep saying that?" Emika asked. "Failure as fuel?"

"It's from that little book you left on the hallway table. The one called *Wolfpack*, by Abby Wambach. Did you know that she won two Olympic medals for the US women's team?" Kaito asked.

Emika nodded. "She held the world record for international goals. For both female and male soccer players. Until the best Canadian player ever, Christine Sinclair, beat her record."

"Anyway," Kaito said, "I was bored the other day waiting for my pottery to dry, so I read it. It's got these eight rules for helping your wolf pack."

Failure

Just when she thought she couldn't feel any worse, something occurred to Emika. Maram had used those words after the game today. *Failure as fuel.* Which meant that Maram had read the book. Which meant that, unlike Emika, Maram was actually trying to use Rosa's gift.

"Abby Wambach says failure is a good thing because, for starters, it means you're *in* the game," Kaito explained. "As long as you stay in the game, you have another chance to do something great. Trust me, I know. You're looking at the master of failure."

"What are you talking about? You win every art award there is at school."

"Do you remember how much I wanted a pottery wheel for two years? I begged Mom, but she said she couldn't afford it. So I worked for two summers washing dishes at the Old Country Restaurant to save up for one. And then when I got it, do you know what happened?" Kaito laughed. "Every piece of pottery I tried to make collapsed on me. And even when it didn't collapse, it turned out lopsided. Sometimes I wanted to give up. I thought I'd never get it right. But those failures couldn't have happened if I didn't have a pottery wheel in the first place. And that meant I was in the game."

"What else does the book say?" Emika asked.

"*Lead from the bench*, that's another rule," Kaito said, squinting as he tried to recall. "I think it means that you're supposed to lead from wherever you are, even if you're on the bench. *Demand the ball* is another rule, if I remember right."

"That's what Maram said to me after she took the corner kick," Emika frowned. "But how is that being a good member of the wolf pack? Going around demanding the ball from your teammates?"

"I don't think the rule means you go around doing whatever you want," Kaito said. "It means not playing it safe. The book talks about how girls especially are taught to do things just to be nice. But don't give the ball to others *just* because it's the nice thing to do. Go for it. Use your talent. Believe in yourself."

Maram definitely doesn't do things just to be nice, Emika thought.

Kaito snapped his fingers. "Oh! I remember the best rule for you, Emika. *Champion each other.* In other words, show your teammates that you're on their side. That one is easy for you. You always seem to know when somebody needs your help. You've really got a great sense of other people, and you know how to pick them up."

I do? Emika wrinkled her nose. She had a great sense of other people? It didn't feel like it lately.

Then she remembered. *You're so good at sensing other people on the field.* That's what Rosa had said to Emika during their last game together.

"But what if I can't show *all* my teammates that I'm on their side?" Emika asked.

Failure

Kaito lifted an eyebrow at Emika. "The rule is *Champion each other*. The rule isn't *Champion only people you like*."

Emika thought about how Rosa didn't just cheer on her own teammates. She cheered on everyone in the game. Like when she patted that Lions goalkeeper and told her how great she was playing. And after Christine Sinclair beat Abby Wambach's goal record, Emika saw a message on TV from Wambach excitedly congratulating Sinclair. Even though they had battled against each other on the field for years.

"But I don't have the words like Rosa or Abby Wambach," Emika said.

"You do, Emika. Even so, you don't always need them," Kaito said. "Wambach says that sometimes all she ever did was point when something good happened on the field. She pointed to the teammate who passed to her. She pointed to the coach who made up the play. She pointed to the players on the sidelines."

Rosa did that all the time, Emika recalled.

Suddenly she felt a small glint of hope.

Kaito winked at her. "You can point, can't you?"

She smiled. "Of course. I can do that."

11 All WASHED UP

Emika arrived at the Nickel Street gas station at quarter after four on Monday. She was relieved when the rest of the team arrived a few minutes later. Nobody had quit the team. Not yet.

She was even more relieved when Jabira said hello to her with a smile.

Once the girls had gathered together, Maram said, "We need four of you to stand on the sidewalk. Get the drivers' attention as they pass by."

"Why four?" Emika asked.

Maram shot her a look. "That way, each person can stand with a sign on one of the four corners of the intersection."

Gabrielle nodded. "Good idea."

"Do we have enough signs?" Emika asked.

Ayana held up a stack of poster boards. "We made six yesterday."

"Emika, you're in charge of the posters and waving down drivers," Maram announced. "I'll be in charge of organizing the rest of team to wash the cars. I brought all the buckets, soap and sponges."

Emika found it easy to take Maram's orders today. She really didn't want to wash cars. She was happy to be walking up and down the sidewalk holding a sign.

While Maram and the others set up their buckets, Emika took Ayana, Jusdeep and Kelly to the intersection. Ayana handed out the posters. Then they each went to a corner.

Although rush-hour traffic was busy, only two cars pulled into the car wash in the first half hour. Kelly walked across the road to Emika's corner. Ayana quickly joined them.

"We have to do something different," Kelly said.

"Like what?" Emika asked.

Kelly shrugged. "I don't know. You're the one in charge."

"I say we dance the Funky Chicken," Ayana suggested.

"What?" Emika shook her head.

"You know, the Funky Chicken." Ayana demonstrated by sticking her hands in her armpits and flapping her elbows. She started to wiggle her hips.

"Okay, okay, I get it," Emika said. "No way."

"Come on," Ayana pleaded. "Don't be a poor sport. Like Kelly said, we have to do something different." Ayana cupped her hands around her mouth and shouted across the street to Jusdeep at the top of her lungs. "We're going to dance the Funky Chicken!"

Jusdeep stuck her arm straight out and gave them a thumbs-up.

Ayana smiled. "See? Jusdeep thinks it's a good idea."

"She probably didn't hear you," Emika said. "She probably thought you said we're going to France to dunk some chicken."

Ayana laughed. "When we're back to our corners, we'll wait for you to start us off," she told Emika.

"Me?" Emika raised her eyebrows.

Before Emika could protest any longer, Ayana and Kelly were already heading back to their corners. Emika looked over at the rest of her teammates, who were washing the second car that had come in. Maram had the team working like a well-oiled machine.

A boy, about fifteen years old, biked up the sidewalk in Emika's direction. She wasn't about to dance the Funky Chicken until he passed. But he turned into the gas station before he got to her.

"Come on, Emika!" Ayana shouted. "Let's do this!"

"How are we supposed to hold up our posters when we dance?" Emika shouted back.

Kelly stuck her poster under her chin and tucked her head down, pinching the poster in front of her body. The other girls did the same.

Emika took a deep breath and thought, *here goes nothing.*

"On three!" Emika held her hand high above her head. "One, two, three!"

In unison, all four girls danced the Funky Chicken. They moved their hands like beaks. They flapped their arms like wings. They wiggled their hips and they clapped their hands. Once they finished the dance, they started all over again without stopping. They did it again and again and again.

Emika felt shy dancing in front of traffic. Her movements were small. Jusdeep and Ayana, on the other hand, danced like they'd gone crazy. Emika could hear Kelly giggling the whole time.

Emika noticed people in cars pointing at them and smiling. One lady in the passenger seat of a big van leaned forward to read Emika's sign, then she motioned to the driver to pull into the gas station. A boy in the back seat of his mom's fancy convertible laughed at the girls' dancing. His mother also pulled into the gas station. Soon, there was a line-up of six cars.

"Two-minute break!" Emika shouted, after they'd danced the routine about twenty times. She pointed out the line-up to the other three girls. Kelly pumped her fist.

Away from the cars, Maram and Jabira talked to the boy on the bike. Although Emika couldn't hear Maram, she could see that her face looked red with anger. She couldn't tell if Maram was yelling at the boy or at Jabira. Maram pointed at the boy and then pointed at Jabira.

Emika felt the urge to leave her corner and see if Jabira needed her help. But just then, the boy got on his bike and took off. As he reached the edge of the gas station, he turned his head and shouted something. He raced up the road.

Emika watched as Maram and Jabira went back to the car wash. Maram grabbed a sponge and Jabira stood off to the side. A couple of times Jabira wiped her cheeks and Emika wondered if she was crying or if she had soap on her face.

"Ready to go again?" Kelly shouted.

Emika nodded, taking one last glance at Jabira.

Raising her arm high again, Emika counted down for another round of Funky Chicken. More cars came into the gas station to line up.

Emika was feeling less shy about dancing now. She loosened up and started to act as silly as Jusdeep and Ayana.

"Woohoo!" Jusdeep pointed at Emika. "Way to go, girl!"

Emika smiled. It felt good when Jusdeep pointed at her that way. It was like an invisible connection between them. It was as if Jusdeep was saying, *I see you and you're an awesome part of this.*

When the car wash was over, the Wolves cleaned up all their stuff and gathered in a group. Maram held the tin of money.

"Good job, Wolves," Maram said. "I won't know

until I count the money tonight, but I think we made a lot."

"Thanks to our dancing!" Jusdeep joked.

Maram looked at Emika. "You did a great job bringing the cars in."

"And you did a great job washing the cars quickly," Emika said.

For a moment, Emika sensed that her team had taken a good turn. No one had quit yet and the car wash was a success. Maram and Emika had even said something nice to each other for the first time ever.

But then Emika looked sideways at Jabira. Jabira was staring at her sister. She looked sad and her eyes were puffy and red.

Emika's good feeling vanished.

If Maram did anything to upset Jabira, she thought, *I will never ever champion her.*

12 Red CARD

The next Saturday was a rematch against the Langford Waves. Ten minutes into the game, Emika dug her cleats into the grass and ran straight at a Waves player. Before the pass could be made, Emika slid along the ground and kicked the ball away. Ayana took it up the field and quickly passed it to Maram in the middle.

"Open!" Emika yelled.

Maram launched a perfect pass to Emika. Emika received the bouncing ball on the inside of her thigh. Pushing past a midfielder, Emika passed it back to Maram and sprinted ahead for a give-and-go play. She cut to the inside and received another pass from Maram.

"Ayana!" Emika shouted as she lobbed the ball softly into an open spot.

Ayana trapped the ball with her foot, then nudged it ahead to line it up for the shot. But the goalkeeper caught the ball with both hands, cradling it in her forearms.

The team's success at the car wash seemed to

have given them more energy on the field. Emika remembered what Kaito had said about championing each other. How you didn't always have to find the right words. She looked at Ayana as they jogged back for the goalkeeper's punt down the field. Without a word, Emika pointed at Ayana. She looked at Maram and for a brief second, considered pointing at her, too.

But then Emika remembered how upset Jabira had looked at Maram at the car wash. So she turned away and ran back down the field.

The Waves goalkeeper kicked the ball, but only got a piece of it. The ball spun off sideways and bounced over the Waves defender's foot and out of bounds. Kelly raced for the throw-in and hurled it straight to Emika. It almost went over her head. Emika jumped and flicked her head backward. Her header sent the ball into the middle.

Maram battled a Waves midfielder for the ball, but it popped away from both of them. Kelly stretched to the ball before anyone else. She made a quick fake to the left and then burst past a Waves player. She fed a short pass back to Maram.

Maram spun around to keep her body between the ball and the Lions midfielder, who was checking Maram like a shadow. Maram leaned into the midfielder and pulled the ball backward with the bottom of her cleat.

"Need some help!" Maram called out. "Let's get open, Wolves!"

The Waves midfielder started shoving Maram in the back. Maram kept control of the ball, even though she struggled against the midfielder's rough play. Finally, the Waves player shoved Maram right onto the ground. Still, Maram didn't give up. Nearly lying down, Maram swung her leg around and launched a pass back to Kelly.

When the ball eventually went out of bounds, Emika made a comment to the referee. "What was that?"

"What was what?" The referee shook her head.

"That was a foul," Emika said. She didn't care that it was against Maram. She was fed up with the unfair play. "They can't shove our players."

"I can only call what I see," said the referee.

Under her breath Emika muttered, "Try opening your eyes, then."

"Let it go," Maram whispered. "Don't get yourself into trouble. We need you on the field, not kicked out of the game."

"We can't let them get away with that stuff," Emika insisted.

Maram shrugged. "The Waves are just frustrated that the game's so tight. Especially after they beat us so easily last time."

Emika nodded. It was nearly half-time and the score was still tied at zero. She still hated to admit she had been wrong, but the short pass game was working for the Wolves.

By the start of the second half, the game was still tied, with neither team able to score. The Waves got rougher as the game went on. Kelly got tripped twice during crowded battles for the ball in midfield. Jusdeep was rushed by a forward long after she'd made the save. The referee didn't give the forward a yellow card, but at least she gave her a warning.

Jusdeep kicked the ball up the field. It soared high over the midfielders' heads. Emika sprinted to get into an open spot. Nearby, a Waves midfielder lunged at Emika from the side. The toe of her cleat went into Emika's thigh, just above the knee.

Emika doubled over in pain. Instantly, a bruise began to form.

"Sorry," the midfielder muttered. "I was going for the ball."

Emika winced. "The ball wasn't even near me."

But the midfielder was already running toward the play.

Emika charged up the field, trying not to let the rough checking get to her. She watched Nina dart to the far sideline and make two beautiful step-over fakes to beat the defender. Instead of sending the ball up the wing, she crossed it into the middle.

Maram trapped it with her chest and let it drop to her foot. She juggled it once, keeping it in the air, then booted it backward over her head. It soared high toward Emika.

Maram must have sprinted as fast as she could, because next thing Emika saw was Maram rushing up the middle, almost even with her. Just as Emika crossed it back to Maram, one of the Waves defenders slid into Maram with her cleats high. Maram's legs kicked out from under her. She went tumbling to the ground.

The Waves goalkeeper grabbed the ball.

Emika ran up to the referee. "No call? Are you kidding?"

The referee put her hand up. "You need to move back. You're in my face."

"So? Are you going to call a foul?" Emika asked, backing up a few inches.

"It was an accidental collision," the referee explained. "It was the fault of both players."

Emika threw up her arms in disbelief. "That's the worst call I've ever seen."

The referee reached into her shirt pocket and held up a yellow card.

"You're giving me a yellow card?" Emika was astonished. "I can't believe I'm getting a yellow card and their player gets nothing for almost injuring one of our best players."

"Watch yourself," said the referee.

"Watch myself?" Emika said. "Maybe you should watch yourself. Maybe you should watch *something* for once."

Red Card

The referee reached into her pocket and held up a red card.

Emika's face fell. A red card? She'd been shown her first red card ever. She couldn't believe it. She was kicked out of the game. She could feel all her teammates watch her as she walked away from the referee. But she didn't look back at any of them. Ashamed, she slunk off the field with her head hung low, her gaze fixed on the grass.

From the sidelines, Emika watched her team play the rest of the game. So far Coach Garcia hadn't commented on the red card. Emika knew she would, in time. But nothing Coach Garcia said could make Emika feel any worse than she did right then. For once Emika had sided with Maram and it had backfired horribly. She could hardly stand to watch the game now.

"Let's go, Wolves, let's go!" Jabira stood nearby, cheering.

Sitting down on a water cooler, Emika rested her chin in her hands. She planned to stay there for the remainder of the game, silent.

The referee blew the whistle to warn everyone there were only two minutes left in the game.

The score was still 0–0.

"Two minutes, Wolves! Push hard!" Jabira yelled. "You can do it!"

As Emika listened to Jabira's nonstop cheering, she couldn't help but smile.

Jabira is the heart of our team, she thought. There was no doubt about it. In fact, Jabira was possibly the most important leader the Wolves had. Especially with Rosa gone. It didn't matter that Jabira wasn't on the field. She could lead the team from anywhere.

Even from the bench.

Emika stood up and joined her. "Let's go, Wolves! Stick with it! Give it all you've got!"

13 The ACCIDENT

When Emika woke up the next morning, all she could think about was that red card. She shouldn't have talked to the referee that way. She replayed the scene in her head. Why had she been so rude? It wasn't like her. She wished she had handled it differently. What would Kaito have to say about it? She couldn't bear to tell him. Deciding that she needed some time to herself, Emika took her soccer ball to the park.

The park was packed with people walking their dogs and with little kids on the playground. Emika found a quiet spot between two cedar trees and juggled the ball with her feet. She flicked it up to her thighs. When she let it drop back down to her feet, the ball bounced forward and onto the ground.

"You have to absorb it with your foot."

Emika spun around. Jabira stood there, holding her soccer ball.

"That's what somebody taught me once." Jabira smiled.

Emika smiled back, remembering the first time she showed Jabira how to juggle a soccer ball. "Feel like passing it around?"

Jabira nodded. Together they walked to a spot in the middle of the field. Emika tossed her ball to the side and waited for Jabira to pass.

"That was some show you put on last game," Jabira said.

Emika trapped the pass, nudged it forward and then kicked the ball back to Jabira. "Please don't remind me. Not the high point of my soccer career."

"I've never seen you like that before." Jabira missed the ball.

"I'm not sure why," Emika admitted. "But I just got so mad." Then she paused for a moment. "Also, I guess I thought it would show some leadership."

Jabira gave her a funny look.

"I went too far," Emika said. "I know it."

"You and Maram are the same that way," Jabira said.

Emika laughed. "Maram and I are not the same in *any* way."

"Both of you are like dogs with a bone when it comes to sticking up for others." Jabira worked on using the outside of her foot to pass it back to Emika.

Emika watched the ball roll slowly toward her.

"Why was Maram so angry at the car wash?" Emika asked. She picked up the ball and did a throw-in so Jabira could practise trapping it.

Jabira let it bounce off her kneecap. "She was mad at that boy —"

"She wasn't mad at you?" Emika interrupted.

"No." Jabira got set to receive another throw-in.

Emika threw the ball. "You looked so upset at Maram that I just assumed . . ."

The ball rolled over Jabira's foot. "Assumed what?"

"That Maram was being mean to you," Emika said.

Jabira passed the ball. "Why would you assume that?"

Emika shrugged. "Because Maram never seems to be nice to you."

"That's not true."

"She never talks to you at soccer," Emika pointed out. She kicked the ball into the air so Jabira could practise trapping it with her body.

"Things aren't always the way you think they are, Emika," Jabira said. She trapped the ball and moved close to Emika. She juggled it back and forth between her feet. "When you see things without knowing everything, you don't always see the whole picture."

Emika didn't listen. She carried on making her point. "She barely even looks at you at soccer. She never plays pass with you. She must know how much you love soccer."

"She knows," Jabira said.

"Doesn't it bother you?"

Jabira put her foot on top of the ball to stop it. She

looked up at the trees for a long moment, lost in thought. Then she gave Emika a serious look and said, "What I'm going to tell you is a secret. You can't tell anyone, okay?"

"I won't." Emika made a crossing motion over her heart. "I promise."

"Do you know how people get cerebral palsy?" Jabira asked.

"I figured people were born with it."

"Some people are," Jabira said. "But some people can develop it from a brain injury when they are very young. Like from a car accident."

There was a long silence between them.

Emika asked in a quiet voice, "You got cerebral palsy from a car accident?"

"I was four years old. Maram was five. We were both in the back seat of the car. A truck crashed into my side of the car. My mom was in the front passenger seat on the same side. She got a dislocated shoulder and a couple of broken ribs. I hit my head hard on the car window."

"What happened to Maram?" Emika asked.

"Nothing. Not a scratch. Same with my dad, who was driving."

Emika had a hard time making sense of what she was hearing. All this time she had thought her best friend was born with cerebral palsy. But she wasn't. Jabira was born healthy. It was terrible to think that a stupid accident caused her condition.

Jabira threw her jacket on the grass as a goalpost. She rolled Emika's ball over to be the other goalpost.

"Take shots on me. I want to be goalkeeper."

Emika took a light shot. "Doesn't it make you mad to know —"

"To know that I might have been different?" Jabira looked at the ball. "Shoot harder."

Emika nodded. She shot the ball a little harder.

Jabira saved it. "If I'd been born this way, it would still just have been bad luck."

"I don't know if I can see it that way," Emika said.

"Neither can Maram." Jabira kicked the ball out of her hands. "Every time Maram sees me at soccer, she is reminded that she can play and I can't. At least, that I can't play in the way she can. She understands that I love to come watch the games. I understand that it's hard for her to see me there."

"So that's why she never plays with you?" Emika asked.

"I don't mind. I have you to play with."

Jabira's words warmed Emika. Still, Emika thought that it must be sad for Jabira that her own sister wouldn't play with her.

"There are other ways that Maram champions me," Jabira said.

Emika tilted her head in disbelief. She'd never seen Maram doing anything for Jabira.

"At the car wash," Jabira explained, "there was a

boy making fun of me. Pretending to walk like me and move his hands like me."

Emika cringed at the idea. She had seen other people making fun of Jabira behind her back and it made Emika's head hot with anger.

"Wish I was there," Emika said. "I would have stood up for you."

"Thanks," Jabira said. "But I can take care of myself."

Emika's cheeks flushed with embarrassment. Emika knew that Jabira hated it when people tried to rescue her. She had been dealing with people like that boy all her life. She had always managed to take care of herself.

"After what I said to that boy," Jabira went on, "he'll never bug me again. Maram was just there for extra support. You know, to show that boy that there are people in my corner."

"I'm in your corner, too," Emika said.

"Yes. You're both in my corner."

Emika stared at the little kids on the playground in the distance. All of a sudden, the Maram she thought she knew changed somehow. Emika saw her in a different way.

Kaito's words echoed in her mind.

It all depends on what you know about a thing. Sometimes a person thinks a thing is a pot, but it's not a pot. It's something else. And sometimes a person thinks a thing is a cup, but it's not a cup. It's something else.

When she looked at Maram she'd always thought she saw a pot. But now she realized that this whole time Maram was actually a cup.

Emika stopped the ball and looked at Jabira. "Sorry about pizza night. I shouldn't have done that. I don't know what I was thinking."

Jabira smiled. "I do. You were thinking that you'd get the team to want you, and only you, as captain."

14 Peanut Butter and CHOCOLATE

Emika and Maram crouched, ready for the whistle. They both stood at the front of a line of teammates. Emika's group wore red practice jerseys. Maram's group wore blue practice jerseys. Far down the field, Coach Garcia put the whistle up to her mouth.

"Ready, red team? Blue team?" Coach Garcia asked.

"Ready!" Emika called out, trying to get her team pumped up.

"Ready!" Maram said.

"Losing team does three laps around the field," Coach Garcia reminded them. "Each team picks one player to go twice. Here we go!"

Coach Garcia blew the whistle. Emika and Maram took off as fast as they could, each dribbling a soccer ball. Weaving between the long line of orange cones, Emika could see that Maram was about a metre ahead of her.

Emika pushed harder, moving the soccer ball from

one foot to the other. When she reached the end of the cones, she sprinted to the goal. Maram was still ahead.

From inside the eighteen-yard box, Maram shot her ball into the net.

A few seconds later, Emika shot her ball from the same spot. It hit the post and bounced straight back. Emika groaned. Emika's missed shot put Maram even farther ahead.

Maram retrieved her ball from the net. She carried it under her arm as she raced back to her team's line-up. Emika booted her own rebound into the net and grabbed it for the last sprint.

Maram set the soccer ball down on the ground in front of Kelly. "Shoot it right away," Maram instructed Kelly. "Just like I did."

Emika put the ball in front of Ayana. "Sorry about that shot," she mumbled.

Ayana shrugged and dribbled the ball toward the cones.

"Go, Kelly, go!" Maram shouted. "You can do it!"

Emika watched Maram. Just like Jabira, Maram led the team from wherever she was, not just on the field. She got the team going on their fundraising and she organized the entire car wash day. She might never smile, but now Emika understood why. If Emika had been in Maram's shoes, if she had a family secret like that, she might not smile very often either.

Just then Ayana passed Kelly in the relay race.

Emika pumped her fist. "Way to hustle, Ayana!"

Kelly noticed she was overtaken by Ayana. She turned the last cone too sharply and fell down on her side. Frustrated, she thumped the ground with her fist.

"It's not the end yet, Kelly!" Maram yelled. "Don't give up! You're still in it!"

Nina caught up to Gabrielle on the next leg of the relay. It stayed a tight race through the next three pairs of racers.

"Last racers!" Coach Garcia shouted. "Pick a player to go for their second time!"

"Me!" Maram told her team, grabbing the ball. "I'll go again."

Demand the ball, Emika thought. Maram didn't play it safe. She believed in herself. She knew how to go for it. If anybody lived by the *Wolfpack* rules, it was Maram.

"I'm going again," Emika said, taking the ball from Ayana.

Both Maram and Emika took off dribbling. At the end of the cones, Maram kicked a long shot into the middle of the goal, then fished the ball out of the net before Emika made it to the last cone. There was no way Emika would catch her.

The blue team won.

"Red team does three laps around the field," Coach Garcia said.

The red team groaned. Emika led the run. Behind

her, she could hear her teammates talking quietly to one another.

"This practice is going better," Gabrielle said.

"Yeah, they're not fighting for once," Ayana said.

"I guess," somebody else said. Emika couldn't quite make out who it was, and she didn't want to turn to look. "But how long will it last?"

"You still thinking of quitting?"

"I don't know. I don't think I can ever trust either of them as a captain."

"Me neither. Only because they don't get along. Maybe we can ask Coach Garcia if just one of them could be captain."

"But which one? Emika or Maram?"

"I'd say Maram."

The words felt like a blow to Emika's stomach.

"Maram knows how to take charge," the voice went on. "We need that. She's good at making decisions and getting us organized on the field. She knows the game so well."

"I agree. She knows the best strategies for all our players."

"Plus, Maram is always trying to help the team out. Remember when she spent all summer practising throw-ins so she could take those? Or when she practised being a goalkeeper in case Jusdeep got injured? And those corner kicks, they really helped us out. She works hard for the Wolves."

Did Emika hear that right? Her teammates believed Maram did all that extra practice for the sake of the team? Didn't they think at all that she was trying to take over?

"She sure does work hard," someone agreed. "And like Rosa always says, Maram sticks with it no matter what. It makes me play harder."

"My mom says that Maram is someone who leads by example. She doesn't *tell* us to play harder. She *shows* us to play harder by doing it herself."

"Emika plays hard, too." That was Jusdeep's voice. "And she makes players feel good about themselves."

"But that fight Emika got into with the ref last game was so embarrassing."

"Everyone makes mistakes," Gabrielle said. "I'm willing to forget about what happened last game. We need a captain as enthusiastic as Rosa. That's Emika."

Emika smiled to herself.

"Emika has always made me feel good about being on the team," Jusdeep said. "She always made me feel that she's glad I'm on the team."

"I can go to Emika about anything," Nina said. "She always makes me feel better."

"She *used* to be like that. Don't you think she's changed since becoming captain?"

"Definitely. She used to be a big part of our team spirit. Almost as much as Rosa"

"And Jabira," added Ayana.

"We need a big heart leading the team," said Jusdeep.

"You know what?" Ayana said. "In theory, Maram and Emika should be perfect co-captains."

You two are like peanut butter and chocolate. That's what Rosa had told Emika.

"Sure, if they got along. But they never will."

"Maybe we could talk to them. Tell them to get along."

"No way. Even if they promised to get along, I wouldn't trust them now."

"Me neither."

Emika turned the last corner of the last lap ahead of her team. She felt a knot of loneliness in her stomach.

I'm supposed to never feel alone, she thought. *Not when I have my wolf pack.*

Emika had to find a way to work with Maram.

And she had to find a way to bring the pack back together.

15 Champion EACH OTHER

By the time Emika got home, she had come up with a plan. At least, the first step of a plan. She fired up her computer and opened the team chat group.

"Okay." She rubbed her hands and whispered to herself. "Now if I can only think up some positive messages. Something Rosa might say."

At first, Emika thought of nice things to say about the whole Wolves team. Like how great they worked together at the car wash. Or how great their passes were getting. Or how amazing they were going to play at the Vancouver tournament.

Somehow Emika knew that wouldn't be enough. The messages needed to be about each player. About what each player brought to the pack. Emika needed to champion her teammates one at a time.

She took out a notepad. On it, she made a list of all the Wolves players. Under each name she left a space for notes about what to say. But everything she wrote sounded like something Rosa had already said.

"I'm making popcorn." Kaito popped his head inside her bedroom door. "Want some? Double butter."

Emika tossed her pencil onto the notepad and flopped back in her chair with a sigh.

Kaito stepped into the room and glanced at her desk. "Homework?"

Emika rubbed her hands over her face. "Soccer. I'm trying to come up with something positive to say to each teammate."

"I'm guessing it's not going well?" Kaito asked.

"It's going terrible," Emika said.

Kaito looked at her notes. "Terrible? Looks like you have some great ideas there."

"But they're not my words. Not really. They're mostly Rosa's words."

"What's wrong with that?" Kaito shrugged.

"I can't just steal Rosa's ideas," Emika said.

Kaito laughed. "Artists borrow ideas from each other all the time. Over hundreds of years, artists have been influenced by each other. One of my favourite artists is Takuro Kuwata. My pottery borrows a lot of ideas from him. Don't just copy Rosa's words and call them your own, but let them inspire you."

"Thanks, Kaito."

Kaito gave her a thumbs-up. "Be back soon with some popcorn."

Emika picked up the *Wolfpack* book from her desk

and flipped through it. She remembered many of the rules from when Kaito had explained them to her. As she browsed through the book some more, Emika still worried she didn't have the courage to follow all the rules. But the more she read, the more she knew that these rules were the answer to her problems.

Between Rosa's words and the *Wolfpack* book, Emika managed to scribble down some ideas. It took Emika another hour and a big bowl of popcorn before she had sent positive messages to almost every player on the team. She described to Jusdeep how amazing it was that she never gave up trying to make a save. She told Kelly all the ways she was smart on the field. She told Ayana how her speed opened up the play and how her smile made everyone feel good no matter what happened. Using Rosa's words for inspiration, she found a way to make every message unique to each teammate.

Now the messages were there in the team chat group for everyone to see.

The only player left was Maram.

Emika thought about how the Kassab family's car accident had changed Jabira's whole life. Nothing had happened to Maram. It wasn't Maram's fault, but Emika could understand how unfair it must feel. Maram had always been unsmiling and seemed cold. But maybe Emika would be the same in Maram's shoes.

As Emika searched her brain for something positive to send to Maram, Jusdeep responded to her message.

Thanks, Emika!

It was a simple message, but it made Emika feel warm inside.

A few other messages *dinged!* into the chat window. Other teammates thanked her.

It's working, she thought. *I'm bringing the wolf pack back together.*

Emika went back to concentrating on Maram's message. If she took too long to add Maram's, it might be obvious that Emika was having a hard time thinking of something to say.

Emika thought about the things her teammates had said about Maram as they ran laps in their last practice. How Maram led by example, showing her teammates that she expected from herself what she expected from all of them. How Maram knew all the Wolves players' strengths and how she could figure out the best strategies on the field. How Maram made great decisions and how she could organize everybody. How she practised everything in order to help the team.

While Emika had to admit they were right about some things, she still thought that Maram was at least a little on the bossy side. Wasn't she? Emika closed her eyes and tried to recall a time when Maram had told her what to do.

That first corner kick at practice. That's what popped into Emika's mind.

"Stand by the goalpost nearest me," Maram had told her.

And Maram had been right. Emika had scored a beautiful header. But being right didn't make Maram any less bossy.

Then there was the corner kick during the game against the Thunder.

"I'm taking it this time," Maram had said. "You need to be next to the post."

She had repeated it. Sort of, Emika remembered. The second time, she'd pointed Emika at the goal and said, "I need you next to the post ready for another header."

Deep in thought, Emika stared at a poster of Christine Sinclair on her wall. Both those times, Emika had heard Maram's words as bossy commands.

In her mind, Emika went over the words again.

I need you next to the post for another header.

Slowly, it dawned on Emika. The corner kick wasn't just about what Maram wanted. It was about what the team needed. Better yet, Maram actually had some faith in Emika. How did Emika not see that before?

We're both good at different things, Emika thought. Just like Rosa had said.

That gave Emika an idea. In the team chat group, she typed to Maram:

You're good at things I'm not good at, and I am good at things you're not good at. We're like peanut butter and chocolate. If we work together . . .

Emika stopped typing. She didn't know how to finish the sentence.

"If we work together . . . we'll be delicious?" she whispered aloud.

Too corny, she thought.

Emika stared at the last sentence for a few more minutes. Finally, she decided to leave it as it was. She hit SEND.

Maram must have seen it right away. Hardly any time passed before she sent a reply to Emika.

What is this supposed to mean? Why did you send this to me?

Emika slumped in her chair. That was not the response she was hoping to get. Instead of saying thank you, like all her other teammates, Maram seemed suspicious of Emika. But why? What did she think Emika was up to?

Emika put her fingers on the keyboard, but she didn't type. She and Maram had spent the last two years not trusting each other. In fact, they'd spent the last two years assuming the worst about each other. Emika could kick herself for her dumb idea. How could she

have thought that a few words would make Maram
trust her all of a sudden?

Emika closed the chat group so she appeared to be
offline. She stayed on her computer, though. She had
to find more ideas for saving the wolf pack.

She searched: *How to build trust on a soccer team.*

It was going to take more than a few kind messages
to bring the pack back together.

16 A Game of TRUST

"I've got it all figured out," Emika told Jabira as they walked to practice on Thursday. Coach Garcia had scheduled two practices that week to prepare for the Vancouver tournament.

"All what figured out?" Jabira asked.

"What will fix the team," Emika answered.

"Great!" Jabira said. "So what's your plan?"

Emika wiggled her eyebrows. "A game of trust."

"A game of what?"

"You'll see. I researched team-building exercises last night," Emika explained.

When they reached the field, they saw Maram helping Coach Garcia place cones across the field.

"I better go help," Emika said, breaking into a sprint.

Emika took the cones out of Coach Garcia's arms and continued to set them in a neat line. "Coach," she said, out of breath. "Can I run one exercise with the team today?

"I don't know," Coach Garcia said. "We have a lot to cover before the tournament this weekend."

"Please," begged Emika. "It's very important."

Coach Garcia studied Emika's face. "All right. But let me run a few drills first."

Emika nodded. "Thanks, Coach!"

They moved through the drills quickly. Coach Garcia started with a give-and-go drill, then followed with a one-touch shot drill. Many players took two or three touches before shooting the ball. As usual, Maram led by example, showing her teammates to work hard by shooting the ball with only one touch. Emika copied Maram, showing her teammates that she was working harder than she ever had before at a practice.

"Nice one-touch shot, Emika! Keep it up!" Coach Garcia shouted.

Emika pointed at Ayana to thank her for the perfect pass.

"Bring it in, Wolves." Coach Garcia motioned for the team to join her. "Emika's got an exercise she wants to try."

Emika froze. She had been excited by her idea on the way to practice. But now she was filled with doubt. What if the team thought it was dumb? What if they laughed at her? What if they refused to do it?

Maram would probably think it was a waste of time. Maybe Coach Garcia would, too.

"You're in charge," Coach Garcia told Emika.

The whole team stared at Emika, waiting.

Emika's voice sounded quiet. "Everyone, get in a circle."

The Wolves shuffled into a big circle.

"No. Closer," Emika instructed.

The players moved inward. They touched shoulder to shoulder.

"Even closer," Emika said.

Finally, the Wolves were in as tight a circle as possible.

"Everyone needs to have their hands up near their shoulders." Emika showed them. "And we need a volunteer to go in the centre. I will blindfold the person. Then the person falls in any direction. The team will keep the person from crashing to the ground."

"Blindfolded?" Ayana asked. "Yikes."

"We're supposed to trust that we won't fall?" Jusdeep asked.

Emika nodded. "Exactly. It's a game of trust."

The team went quiet. As the silence stretched into what felt like minutes, Emika started to get nervous. Maybe no one would participate.

Then Maram raised her arm. "I'll go first."

Emika smiled. She pulled a bandana from the pocket of her track pants and tied it around Maram's eyes. "Put your arms straight down at your sides," Emika instructed. "No matter how much you want to, don't stick your arms out to catch your fall. Trust your teammates."

Nodding, Maram stood at the centre of the circle. "Ready?" she asked.

"We're ready," Kelly said.

But Maram didn't move.

"Aren't you going to start?" Gabrielle asked.

"I'm scared," Maram said.

Emika was surprised. It was hard to imagine Maram scared about anything. It was even harder to imagine Maram would ever admit it.

"Don't worry, Maram," Jusdeep said. "We'll catch you. We promise."

Without any warning, Maram tipped herself sideways like a tree blown over in the wind. With their hands ready, Gabrielle and Nina caught her so that Maram was leaning at an angle.

"Now push her to another spot," Emika said.

Gently, they pushed Maram across the circle. Kelly and Jusdeep caught her and pushed her right away to another section of the circle. Over and over, Maram was pushed around the circle. Always close to falling but always caught by her teammates.

When her turn was over, Maram peeled the bandana off her face.

"What was it like?" Jusdeep asked.

"Really hard at first," Maram admitted. "But after a while I trusted you to catch me." She took a sudden step sideways. "I am a bit dizzy, though."

"I'll go next," Kelly said.

"And then me," Ayana said.

After six players had their turn, Coach Garcia came up behind Emika. The exercise was going to take more practice time than Emika had expected. She gave Coach Garcia a look in apology.

"Take your time, Emika," Coach Garcia said. "This is exactly what the team needs right now. Good thinking."

When all the players had gone into the middle, the team looked at Emika.

"Come on, Emika. It's your turn," Gabrielle said.

Emika tensed. It hadn't occurred to her that she would have to take a turn. Somehow, she thought that if she was running the exercise, she didn't have to take part in it.

"We've all done it!" Kelly said with a smile.

"Are you chicken?" Jusdeep started to dance the Funky Chicken.

"Very funny," Emika said.

"Wait a minute," Maram said. "Jabira should also get a turn."

Over at the sidelines, Jabira was reading through the plays on Coach Garcia's clipboard.

"Jabira!" Maram called out.

Jabira jerked her head in their direction. She looked surprised.

No wonder, Emika thought. *When has Maram ever talked to her at soccer?*

"Come take a turn," Maram said.

Jabira hesitated.

"We want you to try this," Maram said. "The whole team should do it."

Emika tied the bandana around Jabira's head and covered her eyes.

"Are you sure you want to do this?" Emika asked Jabira quietly.

Jabira nodded. "You guys catch me from falling all the time. This is nothing new for me."

"If you're nervous," Maram said. "Fall to me first."

Jabira did just that. She fell face-first toward her sister.

Maram caught Jabira and said, "Trust me."

Then she pushed Jabira to another part of the circle.

Kelly caught Jabira and copied Maram. "Trust me."

Soon everybody was saying it. As Jabira bounced from person to person, all Emika could hear was the voices of many girls saying, "Trust me. Trust me. Trust me."

It was Emika's turn next. There was no getting out of it, she knew. She thought about some of her teammates saying they didn't trust Maram or Emika as captain. Then she thought about how Jabira had joked at the food court about not trusting her own hands to drink from a cup without a bendable straw. If Jabira could trust the Wolves, Emika had to give it a shot.

Maram tied the bandana around Emika's face.

In the centre of the circle, Emika stood like a statue for several moments.

"Don't you trust us?" Ayana laughed.

"Yeah," Maram asked, "don't you trust us?"

Only, Maram wasn't laughing.

Emika made herself fall forward. Just as she thought she was going to crash to the ground, a pair of hands caught her and pushed her to another set of hands.

"Trust me," a voice said.

It was Maram.

Emika was pushed to the other side of the circle. She felt light, as if she was being lifted into the air.

"Trust me," another voice said.

Then another. And another.

17 An Unlikely GOALKEEPER

The first game in the Vancouver tournament for the Wolves was early Saturday morning. They had arrived on the ferry from Vancouver Island the night before. Coach Garcia checked the tournament board.

"Field two." Coach Garcia pointed past the concession stand.

The Chester Sports Complex contained six soccer fields and four baseball diamonds, as far as Emika could see. Teams in matching warm-up jackets wandered the grounds. The concession stand buzzed with parents buying morning coffee.

"Tournaments are the best," Kelly said.

Jusdeep agreed. "It's so exciting! All the games going on!"

"And all the hotdogs going on!" Nina added.

"Tournament hotdogs are the best," Kelly said.

Emika nodded. "Keep an eye open for Rosa, everybody."

"She messaged me yesterday," Ayana said. "Her

team's jackets are blue and red."

"Do we play her team this morning?" Jusdeep asked.

Emika shook her head. "We play the Port Moody Kingfishers first."

Coach Garcia motioned for everyone to follow her. "Let's get to the field and warm up, team."

The Wolves arrived first at the field.

"I'll run the first half of the warm-up," Maram told Emika. "And you run the second half."

Emika gave her a small nod. Maram was still taking charge. But at least she had started offering to share things.

"Let's go, Wolves," Maram said. "Nobody ahead, nobody behind. We warm up as a team."

After the warm-up, the Wolves gathered at the sidelines. Jabira handed out water bottles. Coach Garcia crouched in the centre and drew arrows on her soccer field diagram to remind the team of their new plays.

"Hands in for a cheer," Maram said when Coach Garcia was done. "Wolves on three?"

"No, no," Emika said. "Wolf *pack* on three."

"I like it," Kelly said.

"All right," Maram agreed. "Wolf pack on three. One, two, three —"

"WOLF PACK!" everyone shouted in unison.

Parents and players from other teams lined the sides of the field. That was another thing Emika loved about tournaments: the spectators. She played better when she knew people were watching the game.

Before the opening whistle, they lined up for the kick-off. Emika checked out the other team. They looked pumped and ready to play. But so did the Wolves. Emika had sensed during the warm-up that her team had some of its energy back. Maybe it was the excitement of the tournament.

The game started with some hard battles. The Kingfishers were aggressive on the ball. Soon, the Wolves found themselves on the defensive end of the play.

Their team energy turned into something that seemed like a bad case of nerves. Players were losing their checks. Passes were misread. Then Gabrielle tried to sweep a long ball out of the goal area and missed. The ball rolled over her foot and out of bounds.

The linesperson signalled a corner kick for the Kingfishers.

Emika and Maram hovered above the top of the eighteen-yard box.

"Let's get it out right away, Wolves!" Maram shouted.

"Don't let them get a shot, Wolves!" Emika added.

The Kingfishers forward shuffled toward the ball and launched a high corner kick. All the players near the goal swarmed on the ball when it landed. It bounced back up.

Out of nowhere, Jusdeep leaped into the crowd of

players, her arms stretched high. At the same time, a Kingfishers forward jumped up to head the ball. She thumped her forehead into Jusdeep's nose.

Jusdeep cried out and crashed to the ground. Covering her face with her hands, she squirmed on the grass in pain.

The Kingfishers player rubbed her head, but otherwise seemed okay.

Crouching next to Jusdeep, the referee waved for the paramedics. Emika and Maram made sure everybody gave Jusdeep and the officials enough space.

"It's broken," Emika heard one of the paramedics say. Then he asked if Jusdeep was okay to get up and walk off the field.

When they helped Jusdeep to her feet, Emika saw her nose. It was swollen and bruised already. There was a bump on the bridge.

After everyone clapped for Jusdeep, Emika suggested to Maram, "We should talk to the ref. That was a dangerous play on our goalkeeper."

"I'll do it," Maram said.

"We should do it together," Emika said.

Maram tilted her head to one side, as if she doubted Emika.

Emika sighed. "I'll stay calm this time, cross my heart."

Nina ran up to them. "Who's going to play in net?"

At their games on Vancouver Island, the Wolves

often had substitutes on the sidelines. But only eleven players could make the trip that weekend.

"Maybe one of the defenders?" Kelly suggested.

"No way," Gabrielle said. "I don't have a clue how to play in net."

Emika turned to Maram. "You've practised being in goal in case we ever needed you. Now we need you."

Maram shook her head. "We need me on the forward line. It's going to be tough to score on this team."

Emika hesitated. "I know who we could put in net."

"No way," Maram said.

"What have we got to lose?" Emika asked. "She's already on our team roster."

Maram shook her head. But Emika could see by her face that she was thinking about it.

"She might get hurt," Maram said.

"She might not," Emika said.

"Jusdeep just broke her nose," Maram reasoned.

"If Jabira gets hurt," Emika said, "it would be because she was in the game for once."

Something Emika said must have struck Maram. All of a sudden, Maram marched toward the Wolves' bench. She talked to Jabira, pointing to the net. Then Coach Garcia brought out a spare goalkeeper jersey, which Jabira slipped over her T-shirt.

Jabira walked onto the field.

"They can't be serious," one of the Kingfishers players snickered.

Emika flashed her an angry look.

Another Kingfishers player rolled her eyes. "It's going to take her half an hour to get to the goal."

"Knock it off," Maram snapped. "That's my sister."

"You'll never score on her," Emika told the Kingfishers players.

"What are you saying that for?" Maram whispered. "She's never played in a game. She doesn't even know how to play in goal."

"I take shots on her all the time at the park," Emika said. "Besides, our defenders are going to work harder than ever to make sure Jabira has a good game."

Maram took a long look at her sister, now standing between the goalposts. "What about talking to the ref?" she asked.

Emika shook her head. "Forget it. Let's just go get some goals."

18 Bend It Like MARAM

The Wolves did everything they could to keep the Kingfishers from getting the ball past the Wolves midfielders. When they couldn't push the ball up the middle of the field, the Kingfishers switched strategies. Every time they got the ball, they kicked it far up the wings.

The Kingfishers wingers were fast, and they sprinted hard to chase down the ball. On the wing, Gabrielle struggled to stop the Kingfishers forward from getting a breakaway. So far, she had managed to boot it back up the field or out of bounds. But after ten minutes, Emika could see she was getting tired.

Let's keep it out of our net until half-time, Emika thought. *Then we can regroup.*

The ball went out of bounds in the Wolves' end again. A Kingfishers midfielder wasted no time hustling to the sideline to throw the ball into play. Gabrielle tried to force the winger to the far corner. But the Kingfishers forward swerved to the inside of Gabrielle and charged toward the goal area with the ball.

Every muscle in Emika's body tightened. From her position near the centre line, there was nothing Emika could do but watch. Was it a mistake to put Jabira in net?

Kelly and the other midfielders hurried back to help the Wolves defenders. The Kingfishers forward wound up to blast a shot at Jabira.

Emika wanted to cover her eyes. *Please don't get hurt, Jabira.*

The shot sailed off the ground.

Jabira paused for a second.

Emika recognized that pause. It was like a stutter that Jabira's body made when she tried to move her limbs quickly. Sidestepping toward the shot, Jabira tried to jump. But she managed to hop only an inch off the ground.

The ball soared over Jabira's hand and clanked off the crossbar. It came back down at a sharp angle, smacking Jabira on the side of the head. She doubled over, her hands cupping her ear.

The ball landed in front of her, but Jabira didn't seem to notice.

"Clear the ball! Clear the ball!" Maram screamed at the defenders. She scurried in a panic to the Wolves' net.

Kelly got to the loose ball first. Turning sharply, she kicked it out of the goal area. Nina deked past one Kingfishers player and then another before passing the ball up to Ayana.

Emika started up the field. She glanced back at the Wolves' net. Instead of helping to generate some offence, Maram was in the goal crease talking to Jabira. She had completely taken herself out of the play!

A Kingfishers defender tried to cut off Ayana. Stopping the ball suddenly with the bottom of her cleat, Ayana took a second to survey the field. Kelly also noticed that the Wolves were missing a forward, so she pushed up from midfield and took Maram's spot on the inside position.

Ayana passed the ball to Kelly and sprinted to the goal, looking for a give-and-go pass. Kelly spotted the play and nudged the ball to an open spot, where Ayana picked it up again.

The Kingfishers defenders stayed wide on either side of the field, which left space in the middle of the eighteen-yard box. Emika sneaked across. When no one checked her, Emika charged toward Ayana.

"Here!" Emika called.

Ayana threaded the ball right between a Kingfishers defender's legs. Emika didn't bother to gain control of the pass. Instead, she drilled it straight at the goal.

Thwack! The goalkeeper blocked it with her hands.

One of the Kingfishers defenders tried to clear the rebound from the goal area. But the ball hit the shin of another Kingfishers player and rolled out the side of the goal area.

Emika chased it down. Turning again toward the goal, Emika wound up for another shot from just outside the eighteen-yard box. As she followed through high with her foot, a Kingfishers defender barrelled into Emika's outstretched leg. Emika landed hard on the grass.

The referee blew the whistle and pointed at the Kingfishers player.

"Foul," the referee said.

Emika got up and brushed the grass off her shorts.

The referee placed the ball where Emika had fallen.

"Direct free kick," the referee announced.

Direct free kick, Emika thought. *I could score here.*

Standing shoulder-to-shoulder, the Kingfishers organized themselves into a wall to block the shot. They stood with their hands folded in front of them.

"You got this, Emika!" Ayana said.

Behind her, Emika heard clapping. It was Maram, jogging back up the field. According to the rules, anyone could take the free kick. It didn't have to be the person who was fouled.

Is Maram going to demand the ball from me again?

Emika surveyed the goal, thinking about the kick. She couldn't figure out how to get it past the wall of Kingfishers players. It was like the movie she watched with her teammates, *Bend It Like Beckham*. She wished she could bend the ball right around the wall, like David Beckham.

She couldn't bend it. But she did know someone who could.

Quickly she called Maram over and whispered her plan.

The referee blew the whistle.

Emika backed away from the ball at an angle. She made it look as if she was going to kick it with her left foot. Across from her, Maram watched.

Emika ran at the ball. At the same time, Maram also ran at the ball, following close behind Emika. Emika faked the kick. The wall jumped in anticipation of Emika's shot. From behind Emika, Maram took the real kick.

The ball curved like a banana around the wall of Kingfishers players. The shot took the goalkeeper by surprise. It slipped inside the near post.

"Goal!" Ayana shouted.

"Wow!" Kelly hollered. "Forget Beckham! Bend it like Maram!"

Maram kept her usual straight face. But for a brief moment, the corners of her mouth flickered into a smile.

Emika pointed at Kelly for the great give-and-go play.

Kelly smiled and pointed back at Emika.

Emika pointed at Ayana for the smart pass.

Ayana nodded and pointed back.

Emika pointed all the way down the field at Jabira for helping the team in net.

Jabira pointed back.

Emika pointed at Maram for the incredible shot.

Maram pointed back.

★ ★ ★

At half-time, Maram and Jabira stood apart from the rest of the team. Jabira pointed at Maram, but not in a good way. She wagged her finger, the way she did when she was frustrated.

Emika knew it was rude to listen. Still, she strained to hear what they were saying.

"I'm not made of glass, Maram," Jabira said. "I'm not going to break just because someone kicks a ball at me."

Maram said something Emika couldn't make out.

"You embarrassed me," Jabira told Maram. "Coming down the field like that to talk to me."

"I wanted to make sure you were okay," Maram said.

"But the ball was way down by the Kingfishers' goal," Jabira said. "You left your line without a player."

Maram frowned.

Emika frowned, too. Like Maram, Emika had thought of Jabira as somebody who might break easily.

"I trust you," Jabira said to her sister. "I want you to trust me."

19 Leaders of THE PACK

The Wolves gathered around the tournament board. They watched as the tournament official recorded *1–0, Victoria Wolves* next to their game against the Port Moody Kingfishers.

"Shut-out for Jabira!" Ayana said.

The whole team applauded her. Jabira beamed with pride.

After the first shot that hit the crossbar, Jabira didn't face another shot the whole game. The Wolves midfielders and defenders worked hard to stop the Kingfishers from getting within shooting range. Even so, Jabira deserved the applause. For helping the team out when they needed her. For being much more than their cheerleader. She was a key part of the wolf pack.

Coach Garcia ended a call on her cell phone. "The paramedic was right. Jusdeep's nose is broken. She has gone back to our hotel with her dad to rest."

Everyone looked at Jabira.

"I'm already wearing the jersey." Jabira raised her arms. "Might as well keep me in net."

"Thanks, Jabira!" Kelly smiled.

Gabrielle patted Jabira on the back. "You're the best."

Emika examined the tournament board. It was divided into rectangles and lines to show which teams played each other. Every time a team won a game, they moved to the right of the tournament board. So far, the Victoria Wolves was the only team listed inside the next set of rectangles. They wouldn't know who they would play that afternoon until the game finished between the South Vancouver Hawks and the Maple Ridge Rebels.

A referee ran to the tournament official and handed him a slip of paper. The tournament official added the South Vancouver Hawks to the Wolves' rectangle. Game time would be 3:30 that afternoon.

Ayana squealed. "South Vancouver Hawks!"

"That's Rosa's team, right?" Maram asked.

Kelly nodded excitedly.

A voice called out from behind. "Wolves!"

Everybody turned to see Rosa waving at them. The whole team rushed over to her. One at a time, the Wolves players hugged Rosa.

"We play you at 3:30!" Jabira said.

Rosa plucked at the sleeve of Jabira's goalkeeper jersey. "What's this?" she asked with a smile.

"Jusdeep got injured," Ayana explained. "Broken nose."

"Oh, that's terrible!" Rosa said. "Hope she gets better soon."

"Jabira did great in net," Nina said.

"I believe it," Rosa nodded.

"Are you captain on your new team?" Kelly asked.

"Duh, of course she is!" Ayana exclaimed.

Rosa shook her head. "Actually, I'm not."

Emika crumpled her eyebrows. "But you're the best captain ever."

"The Hawks had an amazing captain already when I joined the team," Rosa said.

"But you loved being captain," Emika protested. "Doesn't it bother you to not be?"

Rosa laughed. "Not at all."

Coach Garcia said, "You don't have be captain to be a leader."

"That's for sure," Emika said. "Look at Jabira. She's the heart of our team."

"Not just Jabira." Maram said.

For a brief instant, Maram glanced sideways at Emika.

★ ★ ★

The Wolves seemed distracted during their warm-up. They were still excited at seeing Rosa and couldn't wait be on the same field as her again.

We need to focus all this energy, Emika thought.

Emika felt scattered herself. She was excited to play against her old teammate. And she was brimming with pride to show Rosa that she had kept her promise. Although she'd had many moments of doubt, Emika now trusted Rosa's choice of co-captains. Not only that, but Emika had also given the *Wolfpack* book a try. True, she hadn't read the whole book yet, but did that matter? She had still made good use of Rosa's gift.

Still, Emika's stomach wouldn't stop churning. Playing against Rosa made Emika nervous. Would Rosa think she was a good captain by the end of the game?

Emika set herself at the centre line. It was the Hawks' possession and Rosa was ready to kick off. The whistle blew to start the game.

The Hawks tried to pass the ball up the middle of the field. Kelly and Nina swarmed on the Hawks, cutting off the open lane. They battled for the ball and finally it popped out to a Hawks midfielder. She sent it sailing up the wing, where another Hawks player managed to carry it deep into the Wolves' end.

The Hawks' offence is too good, Emika thought right away. *We won't be able to stop them from shooting on Jabira.*

Sure enough, the Hawks winger sent a beautiful cross into the Wolves' goal area. From the top of the eighteen-yard box, Rosa sprinted toward the ball, which seemed to hang in the air for several seconds. Without letting it drop to the ground, Rosa belted the ball out of the air.

It was a rocket of a shot. Top corner. Straight into the goal.

The Hawks players cheered. The Hawks parents cheered.

Rosa ran up to Jabira and patted her on the shoulder. From where Emika stood she could see the huge smile on Jabira's face. Emika had worried Jabira might feel terrible about letting any goals in, but she seemed to be enjoying the moment.

Rosa and her teammates jogged back to the centre line.

"Let's get that goal back, Wolves!" Maram called out.

A few minutes later, the Hawks pressed deep into the Wolves' end again. This time, two players beat Kelly and Nina up the middle with a give-and-go play. The Wolves defenders put pressure on the forwards, but it didn't matter. The Hawks' passes were quick and on-target. It looked like an uneven game of keep-away in front of Jabira.

Rosa took a shot. It skidded along the grass.

Jabira stuck out her foot in an attempt to stop it. She got a piece of it with her toe, but it went into the net. Jabira threw her head back in frustration.

"Good try, Jabira!" Kelly shouted.

By half-time, the score was 4–0 Hawks. Jabira had not made a save yet, and the Hawks' shots seemed unstoppable.

"Sorry, team," Jabira said as everyone grabbed an orange wedge.

"You're doing great," Ayana said.

Jabira raised her eyebrows. "I haven't made a save yet."

"The Hawks' shots are incredible," Emika said. "The score wouldn't be any different if Jusdeep was in net."

Maram took a sip of water. "We got this, wolf pack. The game's not over yet."

Several Wolves players nodded. Kelly and Nina clapped.

Two weeks before, the Wolves players would have moped about being down 4–0. They would have acted like a bunch of lone wolves. But now it felt like losing wasn't the worst thing in the world. What mattered was that they were losing as a team. They were together in this.

"We may be down, but we're not out!" Maram said.

"On the count of three," Emika said.

Emika and Maram put their hands into the middle of the team huddle.

"One, two, three —"

"WOLF PACK!"

The Hawks ended up beating the Wolves 6–0.

The Wolves lined up to shake hands with the Hawks players. As each Wolves player shook hands, she said with enthusiasm, "Good game!"

Emika smiled. She had never been so proud of being part of a team.

Many of the Hawks players gave Jabira an extra long handshake.

"Great job, keeper," they told her. "Way to hang in there!"

Afterward, Rosa came up to Emika. "I always knew you and Maram were both strong leaders," she said. "But I wasn't sure I'd ever see the day when you two got along."

"We don't really," Emika said.

"Could have fooled me. The way you two point at each other after a good play. The way you gave up the free kick to her in your game against the Kingfishers. The way you both keep the team's spirit going."

"You watched our game against the Kingfishers?"

"Of course," Rosa said. "I miss the team. The Wolves were the best group of girls I've ever played with. Maybe even better with you and Maram as captains."

"No way," Emika said. "You were the best captain ever."

"Together you and Maram are better," Rosa insisted. "You each bring a different strength to the team. Peanut butter and chocolate."

Emika grinned. "I still don't think we'll ever be friends, though."

"That's okay, right?" Rosa shrugged.

Emika nodded.

It *was* okay. They didn't need to be friends.

As long as they were part of the wolf pack.

ACKNOWLEDGEMENTS

Like many fans of Canadian women's soccer, I held a grudge against Abby Wambach and her USA teammates after the controversial Canada–USA game at the 2012 London Olympics. It wasn't until after I read Wambach's book, *Wolfpack*, that I came to respect Abby Wambach in a new and profound way. The moment I finished the last page, I knew I wanted to write a story in which the girls, like me, embrace the set of *Wolfpack* rules as the key to confidence, leadership and belonging. Thank you, Abby Wambach. And thank you to every girl and woman I've ever played sports with and against. Thank you for the camaraderie, the competition, the commitment.